# MURDER

## AT THE

# INDIAN

# RIVER

## JAY HEAVNER

*Canaveral Publishing*

*Cover design by*
*Fineline Printing, Titusville, Florida*

**All of the author's books can be obtained from Amazon.**

**Braddock's Gold Novels**
*Braddock's Gold*
*Hunter's Moon*
*Fool's Wisdom*
*Killing Darkness*

**Florida Murder Mystery Novels**
*Death at Windover*
*Murder at the Canaveral Diner*
*Murder at the Indian River*

# Dedication

*To my wife and helpmeet,*

*Vivian Heavner*

## Acknowledgments

*Special thanks to my wife, Vivian,
for suggestions, proofing, support, and
editing.*

*Thanks, William Rowland for the first proofing.*

*To all my first readers, Tracy Stephens,
MartyMaltby, Marie Waters Clyde, Donna
Leighton,Cindy Moran, Ann Cessna, Paula
Spina,Rene Hunt, and Marsha Tressler, thanks.*

*And a special thank you to Cathy
Teets, my first publisher for her advice
and help, above and beyond.*

# Prologue

"Where is it? Tell me where it is?"

"Where what is?"

"Don't play stupid with me. You know what I'm talking about." He slapped the bound man hard across the face. "Don't play games with me. You know where it is. You know where it all is."

"Maybe he don't know where it is, Joe."

"Oh, he does, Bernie. I saw him with it. He knows where it all is, and he's gonna tell us where it all is." He slapped the bound man again. "Tell me where it is if you know what's good for you."

"I told you I don't know where it is."

Joe slugged the uncooperative man in the stomach and then pummeled him with his fists. "Had enough? I got plenty more where that came from."

"Joe, I don't think you can beat it out of him."

"I think you're right, Bernie. We need another means of loosening his tongue." Joe tied a rope around the man's arm at the wrist and pushed him in the water. He managed to get his head above the water and looked at Joe, who said, "Last chance before the real fun begins. Tell me where it is, or I'm gonna drag you through the water on this moonless night until you give me what I want," but the man remained mute.

"Okay, have it your way." Joe began to drag the man behind the boat. He stopped after half a minute. "Had enough?" but the man remained silent. "Okay, chump. Have it your way." Joe sped the boat around until he felt a thud, and the line went slack. "What happened, Bernie?"

"He hit something. Stop the boat." Bernie pulled the rope in and found an arm dangling from it. He swore. "Now, what do we do? You killed him."

"Where's the rest? Where's the body?"

"I don't see no body."

For the next hour, they looked, but found nothing.

"What are we gonna do? The boss will go ballistic, Joe."

"I know. We need a cover story. We'll tell him he wouldn't talk and we tortured him to death. Then we weighed down the body and sank it in a deep part of the river. He won't like it, but he knew it could happen. Remember, he did tell us to kill him when we were done."

"Yeah, he did. He sure won't like the truth."

"Trust me. It will work. It's not the first time we had to lie to him."

*Murder at the Indian River*

# Chapter 1

Early January, 1986

 Roger laid in his usual horizontal position in the La-Z-Boy chair on his porch attached to the front of his ancient trailer. A fan stirred the thick and damp summer Florida air and his bushy hair. The man, often mistaken for Sam Elliott because of the resemblance, gently stroked the fur on the back of the tortoiseshell cat on his lap. "Good kitty," he said as she purred. K9, his dog, a Shepherd mix, rested on the cool concrete floor. Abruptly, the dog stood up ears erect and began to make little sounds Roger took to be anxious anticipation of some sort.

 The cat on his lap arose and darted through the little doggie door in the porch's screen door. Roger followed the dog's gaze toward the nearby road. "K9, what's going on?" he asked with some concern.

 A vintage pickup appeared and stopped in front of the trailer. An old black man of about 65 got out of the truck, a beater about driven to death and running on prayers, faith, and desperation. It looked like it was held together with rust, dust, and memories. A person would never know the man driving it was one of the richest men in the county. Roger believed the old man probably had the first dollar he ever made. Lester Johnson opened the gate and began to walk down the lane to where Roger was. "Now I know why you're acting like that, K9. You're eager for the donut treat Lester has for you. You had me worried for a moment. I thought you knew something bad was coming from the way you jumped up. I've had enough bad things happen to me lately, and I don't need any more right now though wishing them away ain't gonna stop something I have no control over."

 "Hello, Roger. Permission to come on board," yelled Lester.

 "Granted, but you know you don't need permission. You're always welcome here."

 A mouthful of pearly white teeth showed against his Lester's face. "I know dat. Just tryin' to be polite." He quickly walked to the trailer.

"Come on in," Roger said. "You sure have a quick pace for a man of your age."

"Yeah, I do. All them years of hard work in the Laborer's Union has kept me strong and healthy. Dat and keepin' my vices to a minimum."

"You? Have vices? What vices? Mother Teresa has more vices than you, Lester."

He smiled, "I wish dat was true, but I got a few that need workin' on like every human on dis planet."

"What brings you here today, Lester? Are you doin' a wellness checkup on me like ole Bill has been known to do? Did he send you here?"

"Nah, I got business with you. Thought I'd wait till afternoon so I'd be sure you were up and about."

"Lester, has Bill been filling your head full of lies? I get up every day by the crack of noon, even when I don't need to," Roger joked. "That Bill drives me plum crazy sometimes."

"That he do, but the man's got a good heart even if his behavior is somewhat like an alley cat at times."

"That's ole Bill for sure. So what are you here for?"

"You got an electric problem in the bathroom, right?"

"I did."

"You did? Did you fix it?"

"No, Lester, I didn't. You remember that big thunderstorm we had recently?"

"Yeah, I do. That one was a doozy. I ain't seen one like that in decades and I seen a lot of storms."

"Well, I've more work for you, Lester. Power's out to about half my trailer. Could you take a look at it and see if you can fix it? If you can, do it. If it's more than you want to tackle, I'll call an electrician. Know any good ones?"

"I do, but I'm a pretty good handyman, jack of all trades. Let me take a look."

"Seen anything of Bill today?"

Lester said, "Yeah, I have. We was talkin', and he got a call. Seems someone found a body in the river down at the Riverfront

2

Baptist Church early this morning."

"What? And he didn't call me for help? Wait till I see him. I'll read him the riot act. What more can you tell me?"

Lester shrugged, "Not much. Some of the men of the church had a prayer breakfast and afterward were doin' cleanup work on the amphitheater area behind the church by the Indian River. They was cutting down the growed up weeds and smelled somethin' bad. That's when they found the body."

"Bill told you all that?"

"No, he didn't, Roger. Whoever was on the radio was kind of a blabbermouth."

"I should say so. When word of that gets out, someone is gonna get chewed on."

"Bill said as much."

Roger said, "I can't believe he didn't call me"

"Ain't you just doin' cold cases? You're still working with Bill and the county?"

"I am. Still not sure what my classification is officially, but yes, I'm still helping them with investigations. Nothing else has come through." He paused and grinned. "Guess there's always beauty school."

Lester looked at Roger like he drank something sour and was trying to keep it down.

"Just kidding," Roger said with a grin, but his expression changed. He growled through clenched teeth. "I'll think I pay ole Bill a call down at the church and see why he didn't include me in this operation. Looks like I got a bone to chew with him. Bill can be a boil on a butt, and I do believe I need to lance this festering. Don't think he's especially gonna like it either."

"You do what you thinks right. I'll look at your electrics and see what I can figger out and fix."

"You do that. You any good at fixing fuses or head gaskets?"

"I fixed a few in my time. Why?"

"Because when I'm done with Bill, there may be a few that need fixin'."

"Oh," Lester said as the gravity of Roger's words sank in. "Maybe I should get to work on the electrics."

"Please do. The circuit to the refrigerator is working, so my food and beer are cold. Help yourself if you like. You did mention you had a few vices. Is beer one of them?"

"It is, but don't tell the Baptists."

Roger laughed, "Yeah, don't tell the Baptists. That's funny. I bet a bunch of them sneak a brew or three when they get thirsty."

Lester nodded. "I'll toast the first one to the Baptists."

"You do that," Roger said. "Now I have an annoying Chief of Police to deal with. You take care. See what you can find out and feed that donut to K9. I know she thinks you forgot. I'll see you." Roger got up from his chair, walked to his vehicle, started it, stopped at the gate, opened it, and soon disappeared down Canaveral Flats Boulevard.

Lester watched as it disappeared. He felt something bump his leg. "Why K9, you sho' are patient. Here's what you've been waitin' for." He pulled a donut in a plastic bag from his pocket and handed it to the dog. The donut went down her throat in about three quick bites. "K9, I bet you didn't even taste it." She barked as she wagged her tail. "Lookin' for more? Sorry, that was the last one. All gone. See, no more." He held out his empty hands. She looked a little disappointed. Lester stroked her head and back.

"K9, you keep takin' good care of him. You done saved his life once. Who knows? You may need to do it again."

She licked his hands.

"Good dog. Good dog."

After a head rub that both seemed to enjoy, K9 walked to her bed and lay down. Her eyes closed, and she was soon asleep. Lester sat down in a chair on Roger's porch. *It sure was a hot day. Maybe that electrical storm had done a number on the trailer's old electrical system.*

Lester picked up the phone receiver on the little table next to Roger's big chair and heard no dial tone, nothing but silence. *No wonder Roger hadn't heard from Bill or anyone else for that matter.* Lester smiled as he thought of Roger giving Bill the third degree for not calling and asking for his help. Bill would fuss right back and tell Roger he had tried to call, but Roger hadn't answered. And then they'd both fuss and growl like two angry dogs. Later, Roger would find out about the phone not working. Lester wondered if Roger would apologize to Bill for the outburst. He would when he realized Bill'd find out about the phone and rub it in Roger's face. Yeah, he would. It would be the lesser of two evils. Lester was sure Roger would come to that conclusion.

*So another body had turned up. It had sure gotten interesting in the little town recently.* He wondered how this case would work out. Better than the last two, he hoped, but he wouldn't hold his breath. Simple things have a way of getting complicated in no time at all.

# Chapter 2

Roger drove down the rutted street known as Canaveral Flats Boulevard. His anger and indignation rose a notch with each pothole he hit. By the time he reached US 1, steam seemed to pour from his ears. *How dare they leave him out.* It would take everything he had in him not to explode and chew the ear off his friend, Canaveral Flats Chief of Police Bill Kenney.

As he drove the short mile up US 1, his temper cooled to just below the boiling point, but Bill Kenney was still going to get blasted. As he made a right off the highway to the church parking lot, he noted tire skid marks, broken glass and plastics, and fluid spill spots in the southbound lanes. It looked like there'd been another accident.

He drove through the parking lot past the church to the large two-story concrete building where the office was located. As he exited his vehicle, he heard a voice call out, "Roger."

Roger looked toward the sound and saw Pastor Phil Nassey. The pastor had a slight smile on his face. "Good to see you, Roger. Guess you're here about the body?"

Less than pleasant thoughts ran through Roger's mind. *The body? The dead one or the lowlife Bill Kenney who hadn't informed him of the situation or felt like asking for his expert help?* Roger tried to suppress his anger and not growl like he wanted to. "Yeah, I'm here about a body. Word got to me of a development behind the church, so here I am. What can you tell me that might be helpful?"

"Not much. About ten men had a prayer breakfast in the Fellowship Hall early this morning. Two men were cleaning up inside, and the rest went to work around the church and grounds. Some were painting, and some were mowing grass. Charlie Yates and his son Carson were cutting overgrown vegetation down by the Indian River when they smelled something bad, and it wasn't the usual smell of rotting seagrass. Carson chopped his way toward the smell and found the body barely sticking out of the water.

"They told me. I took a look. It's pretty bad. I've seen my share of dead bodies in the twenty years I was a deputy before becoming a pastor, and this one was a real stinker. My guess is it's been in the river a few days. It looked to me like it reached the point of decomposition where gases form inside that caused it to rise from the bottom and then the east winds blew it to the shallows by our amphitheater where we have our Easter Sunrise Services. That's my two cents for what it's worth."

"Thank you, Pastor. That's helpful."

"Let me show you the way to where all the excitement is," Pastor said.

"That won't be necessary," Roger said. "I'll just follow the smell."

"Come with me."

Roger could see the pastor wasn't taking no for an answer, so he followed Pastor Nassey around the building, past a mower sitting in a half-cut area behind the church, around the bleachers, and down a steep bank to a flat area by the river. Yellow crime scene tape stretched across their path. Roger saw the white Safari van of the coroner parked nearby. Its side and back doors were open. "Stop!" a voice cried out. "Don't come any further if you know what's good for you."

The voice seemed to be coming from behind a tree. With a questioning look, Roger turned to the pastor. The pastor shrugged his shoulders and gave Roger an "I don't know," look. A man in a Titusville Police Uniform came from behind the tree, and he was pulling up his zipper. "Oh," he said, "Pastor. Sorry about yelling, but you caught me while I was busy. It's just me here guarding the line. I can't leave, and I had to go or explode. You guys need to see what's going on?"

"Schumer, we do. Mr. Pyles is here to see Chief of Police Bill Kenney," the pastor said.

Schumer said, "Are you the Mr. Roger Pyles who helped solve the Missy McCoy murder case?"

"I am." Roger realized this had to be the same officer Bill had described as useless after he was reduced to a retching fool on seeing his first homicide victim.

"And weren't you involved in the Death at Windover case?" Schumer asked.

"Yeah, that was me."

"Well, let me shake your hand and congratulate you on the fine work, Mr. Pyles." Schumer stuck out his hand.

"Considering where that hand has just been, I think I'd like to take a rain check on the handshake for now."

A puzzled look appeared on Schumer's face. It took a moment for Roger's statement to sink in. "Oh, yeah," said Schumer. "Another time would be better. Just the same, it's good they sent a real pro out to take a look at this."

Roger bit his tongue and said nothing.

The pastor said, "Why do you say that? Did you see something that could be useful in the investigation of this suspicious death?"

Schumer said, "Nothing concrete. It's more of a feeling, you know? It seems kind of suspicious another body turning up so close to where Stiltsville was. It was quite an event when it burned down with all the fire and shooting. I don't think they ever accounted for the body of the one man who lived there."

"No," Roger said, "but I doubt from what I've heard so far that this new body is the one you're referring to. With all the time that's passed, there wouldn't be much more than a skeleton left of him. The Florida heat and aquatic life would have taken care of the flesh by now." Roger sniffed, "This one is too fresh. You'll learn these things if you stay in police work."

"Oh, yes sir," Schumer said. "Thank you for that tidbit of advice, Mr. Pyles. I'll remember it."

"I hope you do, young man," Roger said. "Police work is not for those with a weak stomach. It can take a lot out of you, young fella. If you don't remember every day that you're out there to help and try to make a difference, it can eat you up. I've seen cops get cynical, depressed, and even take their own lives because they let it get to them. Don't let it happen to you, Schumer. Do the right thing. Think. Don't follow the crowd when it's easy. Believe in justice and do the right thing each and every time."

Roger could tell from Schumer's expression he had made an impression on the young man. "Thank you, sir, for that advice, sir. I'll remember it."

"Good," Roger said. "Remembering it's the easy part. The devil is in the details and implications. Now, after my sermonette and its discussion, can we **please** pass and see the possible crime scene? I'm growing impatient. I need to see the body."

"Sorry," Schumer said. He grabbed the yellow tape in his hand and raised it. "Come in and see if you can find something of interest."

Roger gave the pastor a knowing look. They ducked under the tape and walked to where two men were working. Roger said with a grumble, "Bill, I've been looking for you." He would have said more with added heat, but he contained himself because of the pastor's presence. "Why wasn't I invited to the shindig?"

# Chapter 3

The two men bent over an object in the river covered in maggots and flies. They wore rubber gloves, Tyvek suits, and high top boots. One was Chief of Police Bill Kenney, and the other was the county coroner, Will Corbett. They rose from their unpleasant work of examining the putrid body and looked with disgust at the interlopers, one in particular. Bill Kenney said, "Why weren't you invited? Well, if you'd ever answer your phone, you might learn a few things about what going on in this world."

Roger growled, "You didn't call me, you galoot. My phone ain't rang in days. No one's called me about nothin'. I ain't even had any annoying calls from condo salesmen or cemetery plot salesmen."

"Could it be Mister Smartypants, that maybe your phone's not working?" Bill growled back. "I've tried for several days to reach you, and you never picked up, not once. And I'm not the only one. Agent Hernandez has been on my back like a five hundred pound gorilla wanting to know what's up with you. You won't answer your phone for her either. When did you get your last call, Sherlock?"

Roger thought for a moment. "I guess it was before the bad electrical storm we had. It did screw up the power in my trailer. Got Lester over there right now taking a look at it. I guess it could have messed up the phone line too."

"You think?" Bill said. "It don't take a rocket scientist to figure that out. You could have picked up the receiver and checked to see if you had a dial tone."

Roger grimaced. "Yeah, I guess I could have. I just thought maybe people were avoiding me or didn't need me."

Bill rolled his eyes. "I can't imagine why."

The coroner laughed. "Well, now that you're here, why don't you help us?"

"Okay. I see you got up the crime tape. Did you look for footprints before you two tromped right in?"

Bill looked at Will and then growled at Roger. "We did. Only footprints belonged to the discoverers. We matched their shoes with

10

the footprints. It was just like they said. They saw something, checked out what it was, got scared, and got out. This ain't our first rodeo, Roger."

Roger asked, "Where's the camera. Ain't you taking pictures of the possible crime scene?"

Now it was Bill and Will's turn to grimace. Will said, "How about getting my camera out of the van and taking some shots?"

"I'll do that," Roger said. He found the camera and was quickly at work. "What have you got so far? The smell tells me the body's in bad shape."

"It is. Blowfly maggots galore and flesh flies too," the coroner said.

"I've had a little experience with bodies in water in hot climates," Roger said. "I'd guess its history is something like this from what I see and smell. It's been dead for several days in the river. A possible drowning?"

"Could be. I won't know till I get him and I think it's a him from my first observation. The local fauna has been busy doing their job as nature's cleanup agents," Will Corbett said. "I can tell there's trauma to the body and he's missing an arm. It seems to have been ripped from his shoulder, which is funny. A gator would have twisted it off, and it wouldn't have looked like this."

Roger said, "That is odd. Guess you'll have to wait for answers till you get him to the lab and do a proper autopsy."

"I believe you're right on that," the coroner said.

"Hey," growled Bill. "If you're really here to help, how 'bout doin' more than taking pictures?"

Roger and Will looked at Bill, who had a sour and disgusted look on his face. "Yeah, Roger," the coroner said, "Why don't you join the shindig, the nitty-gritty? We've got lots of great smells, decaying bodies, and puke from Schumer. Wonderful sights like maggots and flies and God only knows what else we'll find during the autopsy. It's hot. The sun's beating down on us. The mosquitoes and no-see-'ems are biting. Who could resist a good time like this?"

Roger said, "With an invitation like that, how could I resist? I'm in. Where's the protective gear like you're wearing?"

"It's in my van," the coroner said.

"I'll get it and be back to help," Roger said. He turned to go, but turned back and asked, "Did Schumer really throw up?"

Bill shook his head. "Every time he sees a dead body. And blood. Can't forget blood. That's why I gave him the job of guarding the line."

"How's he keep his job?" Roger asked.

"Friends and family in high and low places," Bill said.

Roger said, "That explains a lot."

Bill, the coroner, and the pastor who remained silent all nodded knowingly. Roger said, "Hey Pastor, you were so quiet, I almost forgot you were here. Do you want to join in the fun? I'm sure we could find something for you to do."

Pastor Nassey said, "I think I'll leave the forensics work to you three Musketeers. I prefer working with the living."

"Pastor, you're being kind," Bill said. "More like the Three Stooges."

The men laughed at the little jab. A little levity, gallows humor, helped in challenging situations. The pastor said, "Hey Bill, I know you talked with the two men who discovered the body, and I know you're up to your elbows in yuck here, well, they have to be leaving. Seems they've got to go over to Fort Christmas and do a demo on making cane syrup from sugar cane for Old Time Days. I'll see if they can remember anything of importance. When I was at the sheriff's department, one of my specialties was helping get information out of both cooperative and uncooperative subjects."

"You never had to strong-arm anyone for information, did you Pastor?" Roger asked.

"No, I never did, not that I didn't want to sometimes," the pastor said. "I never did. You ask some leading questions, get them to trust you, and then they'll usually open up, but some would clam up and say nothing. Hey, I gotta go catch those guys before they leave. Have fun fellas."

"Oh we will, haha," said the coroner. "It's a dirty job, but somebody has to do it."

Bill and Roger nodded, and the pastor left quickly.

Roger got on the necessary gear and was soon at work helping the other two men. More pictures were taken. Samples of maggots were gathered. Some were collected alive, and some were placed in jars of alcohol to preserve them. A thorough search of the area was done, but it turned up nothing significant. They found an old tire, some decaying beer cans, driftwood, and a concrete block, but little more. After this, they maneuvered the smelly body into a body bag and took it to the van for transport. They dismissed Schumer who did not hang around for more. All three men removed the protective clothing and got back into their normal garb. The coroner drove the van up the bank from the river and soon disappeared down US 1.

The pastor met Bill and Roger as they rounded the corner to the church. "All done, guys?"

"For now," Bill said, "though we may have to come back later if need be. I hope not, but we might. Well, leave the crime tape up for now."

"Okay," said Pastor Nassey. "I'll try to see to it that we keep people away from the area where the body was found."

"Please do that, Pastor," Roger said.

"Oh, one more thing, boys. I talked to the Yates, and they told me they thought a boat way out in the river was shadowing them when they found the body. We went up to a second-floor room of this building and took a look with my binoculars. Sure enough, it was still there. It took off when you guys left the river. I thought it could be important."

Bill said, "That is curious and interesting. Could you see who it was or what kind of boat they were in, Pastor?"

"There were two men, maybe three. We couldn't tell for sure. It was hard to get a good look at them from this distance. The boat looked like a run of the mill 16 to 18 footer, but when it took off, it was easy to tell it had a big outboard the way it sped away."

"Thanks, Pastor. That could prove to be significant," Bill said.

Pastor said, "You guys keep in touch, and if I hear or see anything, I'll give you a call. And guys, you know you're always welcome here. Stop in for services or to talk if you need to."

"We will," they said in unison.

"Thanks," Bill said.

"Yeah, thanks," Roger said also.

They walked to Roger's vehicle. Roger said, "Hey, sorry for

the comment about not being invited to the shindig. I'll check on the phone and make sure it gets fixed."

Bill said, "I'll see Ernie the phone man gets over there ASAP. He still owes me a couple of favors."

"Doesn't everyone around here owe you a favor or three?"

"Yeah. Including you, Roger."

"I know. You won't let me forget it either, Bill."

"Had any more rattlesnakes in your mailbox lately?"

"Nope and don't want any either."

"Keep in touch, Roger. Things seem to be poppin'."

"I know, and there's something about this I don't like."

Bill nodded. "I know. I got that same bad feeling. Something's not right, and it's about to go south."

"Yup, something's just not right with this situation, and it worries me."

Bill said, "Yeah, me too."

# Chapter 4

A white van pulled up in front of Roger's old trailer. K9 got up and began to bark as a man exited the vehicle. Roger recognized him as Will Corbett, Brevard County coroner. "He's okay, K9." She quit barking and looked at him for more instruction. "No, I don't know what he wants. I guess we'll find out soon."

The words seemed to reassure the dog. She continued to watch as he hopped the gate and walked down the lane to the trailer. Her ears were erect and alert. She panted slightly. The Florida heat and her wavy coat made her uncomfortable and lethargic in the afternoons, but this was still morning.

Roger yelled, "Hey, Will. What's up? I hadn't expected a house call. It's been several days since I saw you. What's shakin'?

"I tried to call, but you didn't answer your phone. It's just as well. I need to talk with you, and it's pretty important."

"Okay. Come on in. You said you called and I didn't answer. The phone's not rang in a day or two. I've had a local man and a phone repairman look at it. It was working, but I guess something else has developed. How your day been?"

"It's been one of those days. I hired two young nurses part-time to help at the morgue. I think the girl will work out, but don't think the guy will be back."

Will said, "He bailed when we had to take the body out of the vinyl bag to do an autopsy. He was a real wuss. A body starts to sweat when it's removed from the cooler. When we rolled the body on the table, he was nearest to it and got splashed. After throwing up in a trash can, he cleaned up and left. He's not coming back."

"Must be hard to get good help. Did the young gal work out?"

"She did very well for a first-timer. The scalpels and hardware tools we use like pruning shears, razor knives, hammers, and Black and Decker saws used in the autopsies didn't affect her at all."

"That's a good first sign. Where do you get your tools, Will?"

"Travis Hardware in Cocoa, where else? They've been around since around 1885. Ain't nothing they can't get. We got the John Doe on the table and guess what? He had a big erection. It was weird. She laughed I think out of surprise, and it was an uncommon and uncomfortable situation. She was good. I opened the chest and removed the internal organs. Then we had to work on his genitalia. I knew he had to have a pecker implant, and I could ID him from the numbers the manufacturer put on it. I knew this condition meant he had nerve damage to the affected area or heart problems. That's why during a physical, doctors ask us guys if we can get it up. A dead pecker is a good indication of heart problems."

Roger said, "I didn't know that. Sure hope when I get old enough to join the dead pecker club I can accept it gracefully."

"Me too. This guy went through a lot of pain to have it installed. They put a reservoir above the bladder, an inflatable cylinder up the length of the penis, and a pump in the scrotal sack next to the testicles."

"More information than I needed to know, Will."

"A bar fly I knew from Orlando like to whip it out at the pubs and demonstrate. He had other problems besides a dead male organ. Anyway, we had to remove the testicles to get to the pump and the manufacture's ID on the unit. You ever had to do that?"

"No," Roger said. "And I hope I never have to."

"You're right on that. Here you are with your arm in a hollowed-out human canoe pulling away. It was like yanking on a bungee cord. I gave one last tug, and a testicle at the end of the cord came flyin' out and smacked poor Jessica in the forehead. She took a few awkward steps back. I said to her, 'Well Cinderella, you had a ball, and I see you can dance.' Morgue humor is not for everyone. She laughed. Like I said, she was a trooper. Cutting the skull open and removing the brain didn't bother her either. The only thing that did was when I stuck a syringe in the eye to get fluids. It's funny what makes people squeamish."

Roger felt like he was going to be sick. "Yeah, it is. Sounds like she's a keeper."

"I think she's gonna make it. I need help."

Roger said flatly, "Yes, you do. You got anything new on the body we worked on down at the river behind the church?"

Will nodded. "I do. I thought you might want to change the

subject. We may have something big on our hands, but I could be wrong. It's why I came out to see you today. I need to bounce some ideas and facts off of you, no testicles."

"Thanks for that favor."

"You're welcome," Will said. "I give my thoughts and then you give yours. Fair enough?"

"Sounds fair enough. Care for a beer?"

"I would, but I'm on duty," Will said.

"I won't tell if you don't."

Will smiled. "Okay. I could use something to steady my nerves."

Roger got a couple of beers from his refrigerator and gave one to Will. Roger was puzzled what could possibly upset Will after imagining what other gruesome tales he could tell. Two psshhtt sounds followed by gulping sounds followed by sounds of satisfaction filled the screened Florida room.

Roger said, "Nothing like a cold beer on a hot day to cool a man's thirst. I have a question I'd like answered before you start with your spiel on the dead man at the river. You told me you started working with the dead while you were in the service in Vietnam. Some places have an MD for the work you're doing now and call the job Medical Examiner. What arrangements do you and the county have about your qualifications?"

Will said, "The county has kind of grandfathered me in. Most of my training has been on the job. I've got years of experience, and I've been trained by Bill Bass, who runs the forensic center up in Knoxville, Tennessee. I happened to meet him while he was down here vacationing, and I was one of the lucky ones to get in the forensic classes he was developing."

"Don't they call that place the Body Farm?"

"They do and other colorful names like BARF, the Bass Anthropological Research Facility. That's the place, the National Forensic Academy officially. A Mr. Bass was the founder of the lab. The first time you get there and smell the place, you understand where the BARF comes from. I probably know more on the forensic than most MDs, but I just don't have the fancy letters behind my name. As long as I do good work and keep my nose clean, the county seems happy with that arrangement. It works for me. Maybe someday, they'll tighten up in the future."

"Yeah, I've noticed they seem to be a little loose on some things. Like my official unofficial status as an investigator."

"My advice is to go with the flow. Things have a way of working themselves out," Will said.

"Thanks. I could tell you had additional training. You're much more competent than most of the coroners I've run across and a lot of the Medical Examiners."

"Thanks."

"Now, tell me, what's got you all fired up and concerned, Will?"

"I hardly know where to start, so let me start from where we left off two days ago. It's an unfortunate fact, but finding a body in the Indian River isn't an uncommon event. It's a scenic and beautiful place for recreation and fun, but like any body of water, there are dangers.

"Drowning is the most common cause of death. Most deaths can be traced back to careless swimming, boating accidents, and I've even seen cases where people drowned trying to escape the police. Now, back to why I'm here. I took the dead man to the morgue and got our John Doe ready for an autopsy. I examined the deceased exterior and noticed some odd things. The missing right arm had been jerked out and off, not torn off like by a shark or gator. The same side was heavily damaged, several lacerations and broken ribs. I think he was possibly being drug through the water by a boat, and I think he hit an obstacle in the water. When that happened, the body hung up and the arm attached to a rope from the boat was torn off. The dead man then sank, and his tormentors couldn't find the body in the murky water."

Roger said, "Not a pleasant way to go. There're a lot of posts in the water behind the church where Stiltsville burned to the waterline. That's probably what he hit. What do you think?"

Will nodded, "There were some shards of wood embedded in the right side of the body. I'd say that was most likely what happened to our victim."

"Assuming that's the correct scenario, now the question is, who done it and why. Did you learn anything more in your autopsy?

Was he dead when he was being drug around or alive? What did you find, Will?"

"There was some water in his lungs, but not enough to kill him. The trauma to the body, specifically his side, was what killed him. He died when he hit the something in the water, and the evidence does point to something like a wooden post. Now, here's where it gets really interesting."

"Will, you got my attention. What else did you find?"

"I did the standard autopsy. I looked at his internal organs and structure. It all pointed to what I told you so far. What got my attention was what I found in his stomach. The stomach and contents were pretty nasty as I'm sure you can imagine."

Roger nodded. "Nasty is being kind. A billy goat would puke from the smell."

"You got it. Among all the decay and yuck was something hard."

Roger said, "Could you get to the point? You're killing me with suspense. What did you find?"

"An emerald."

"An emerald?"

"Yes. A large green emerald."

Roger scratched his chin. "Not something you normally find in a dead man's stomach."

"No. It's not, but it does answer a few questions to some things I've seen over the years."

"How so?"

"I saw that emerald or one very much like it once before. The emerald was large, almost ¾ of an inch by ¾. Ones that size are extremely rare, and this one had a deep green color that tells me it could only have come from the mines in the mountains of Peru."

"Where did you see it and when?"

"I walked in on my father when he was looking at it at our house. After my mom died, he had only two interests, taking care of me and treasure hunting. He concentrated on the lost booty from the 1715 Spanish Fleet. Ever hear of it?"

"Just a little. Fill me in."

Will said, "Let me give you some history. As you probably

19

know, Spanish conquistadors followed Columbus. These men conquered much of South America and Central America and some of the islands in the Caribbean along with Florida. Spain never had much industry like her northern neighbors, why I don't know, but they didn't. Spain became very rich from the gold, silver, and gemstones they took from the New World. Every year a fleet of ships would leave Spain loaded with supplies needed in the colonies. These were used to get more gold and silver and other items to send back to Spain. The fleet did a big clockwise circle in the Atlantic that took a full year, sometimes longer, to complete. Another fleet in the Pacific brought goods to the Spanish colonies in America from Asia. These goods were transported overland either across Mexico or Panama and eventually they too found their way to Spain."

"That's interesting," Roger said. "So connect the dots for me. What does this gemstone have to do with our dead man's condition and demise?"

"In late July of 1755, a Spanish Fleet of 12 or 13 ships was on its way back to Spain when it ran into a hurricane off the Florida coast. All but one of the ships wrecked on the Florida coast somewhere between Stuart about a hundred miles south of here and Cape Canaveral. Those in the know believe at least half of the ship's wrecks are just offshore. Some were never found."

"Keep going. This is getting interesting."

"The War of Spanish Succession had raged for 13 long years before in Europe and had left the Spanish national treasury in dire straits. The fleet was filled and overflowing with wealth sorely needed by the new King of Spain. His wife had died sometime before, and he'd taken a new Queen. This woman had demanded a huge dowry in gold and precious jewels and until she got it, refused to consummate the marriage."

"Hmm. I can see why the King was anxious about the successful return of the fleet," Roger chuckled.

Will laughed too. "Let's say he was motivated. Anyway, the fleet sank on the local Atlantic coast with a loss of all the treasure in gold and silver and also what has come to be called the Queen's Jewels."

"Kinda like the Family Jewels, eh?"

Will rolled his eyes. "Queen's Jewels sounds better, but I'm sure the King was concerned about the Family Jewels. Over half of the men, women, and children aboard the ships died, close to 1000 people. Many more died afterward because of the horrible conditions the survivors had to endure."

"How bad was it?"

"Little to no food and water. No shelter from the weather and sun. Mosquitoes that would carry you away or drive you mad. Hostile Indians. And the closest rescuers were north over two hundred miles away in St. Augustine or even further away in Cuba. It was a hellish time for those fortunate enough to live through the storm."

"Was any of the lost treasure recovered?"

Will said, "As you can imagine, Spain desperately needed and wanted the booty that went down in the sea. They did a recovery effort on the wrecks they could locate, about half of the ships that started, for several years and claimed to have recovered 80% in spite of the lack of any kind of diving equipment, storms, and pirates. Many people in the know believe no more than 30% of the gold and silver, probably less, was ever recovered."

"What about the Queen's Jewels? Did the King ever get lucky with his new bride?"

"There is no record that any of her dowry was ever recovered. But the couple must have worked something out. They went on to make many little monarchs. My guess is the new Queen realized that she wasn't of much worth if she produced no babies. Their royal children were of great value in buying alliances with other nations in Europe. They needed heirs to sit on the various thrones throughout the continent. Kings had been known to get rid of Queens who produced no heirs at all or even heirs of the wrong sex. Sometimes it was a quiet disposal, but other times, she lost her head literally."

"Very interesting," Roger said. "Being royal wasn't always so royal. And let me guess, you think this emerald could be part of the missing Queen's Jewels?"

"I do. I'm almost certain of it."

"Why?" Roger said. "What makes you so sure?"

"There's a little more to my story, and I have something for you to see. Afterward, I think you'll agree with me, but I warn you.

People will kill for this information and already have."

Roger grinned. "With an introduction like that, how could I refuse?"

# Chapter 5

Will handed Roger some yellowed papers.

"What's this?" Roger asked.

"Some papers I found while cleaning out at my father's house after he died. I think it's important. It relates to our dead man."

"Now you have got me curious," Roger said.

"Read, and you'll understand more."

"Okay," he said, and began reading. "I, Miguel Brazo, swear to you that all I tell you here is true. I swear by the Blessed Virgin, mother of Jesus. I am an old man and know I will soon die so I must tell you this tale of my lust for treasure and wealth and give you a warning." Roger stopped. "Is this for real?"

"Read on," Will ordered.

"Okay," said Roger. He started again. "I was born somewhere around 1700. I do not know the exact year or the date. My birth was not important enough to record. I know it was in a small village some miles inland from Seville, Spain. My father died soon after I was born, and my poor mother joined him in death when I was about ten years of age. Before she died, she told me to find my way to the sea and seek my fortune there. She said everyone was getting rich in the New World and I should try to stowaway on a ship going there at the seaport in Cadiz. I was to stay hidden until the ship was far from shore and then appear. People who did this rarely were thrown overboard and the ship would usually find jobs for them to do. Spain never had enough seamen, and she depended upon the fleets to fill her treasury from gold and silver from across the sea. A young man could become wealthy there," Roger stopped. "Okay, Will, if this is a Spaniard's letter how comes it's not in Spanish?"

"If you look at the notes on the second page, you will see a note that states, 'Translated from papers found at Stetson University, Deland, Florida by someone, but the name was illegible. It looks to me like water or coffee damage."

Roger turned to the second page and saw the note. "I see it. So you think this paper is real?"

"I do. My father, the treasure hunter, was healthy up until the last few months of his life. When he got sick, he went downhill really fast. I had to put him in a nursing home. While he was there, someone ransacked his house. The cops thought it was crooks taking advantage of the situation, but I thought it was more. The place was too torn up and had been searched thoroughly. I think the searchers were only partially successful in finding what they were looking for. I think they found the emerald my father had, and it's likely the one I fished from our dead man's stomach. I found these papers in Dad's Bible. I almost missed them. Read on, and things will become clearer."

Roger cleared his throat and spoke the written words. "The weather was warm that day in May when I made my way on board. It was easy to fall in the line of workmen at the wharf and grab some bundles. I carried them deep into the ship and slipped away from the workers in the dark interior. I tried to stay unnoticed, but was found by a sailor after being aboard just two days. Fortune was smiling on me. Sebastian was a pragmatic and practical man and found me a job as the boy who every half hour had the duty of turning the hourglass, a very important job. I did it well, and he soon found me other work to do. He showed me around the ship and explained how it worked. The captain, not a kind man, saw me one day and demanded to know who I was. Sebastian told him I was his brother, and that satisfied the captain. As I had no idea what my last name was, I took his and have used it all my life.

"Our ship, one of six in the Flota or fleet, sailed down the waters of the west coast of Africa. The ship I was on was a naos, a merchant vessel, one of two in the fleet. There were two warships for protection plus a patrol vessel and a supply ship. We passed some islands that Sebastian informed me were known as the Azores. At a point the crew seems to know well, they turned the ship west in the ocean currents and the trade winds that would carry us to the New World. Two months later, we sighted Trinidad and entered the Caribbean. The fleet continued on to Cartagena to take on South American treasure such as gold, silver, precious gems, and pearls. This took some time, but each day the ships grew fuller, but never quick enough for the captain or the fleet's commander. After much delay, the fleet left for Havana where we were to meet up with another fleet of Spanish vessels similar in size. This fleet was full of treasures from the Orient that had been transported across the Pacific by sea and then overland by mule train across Mexico. Here both fleets would take on fruit and vegetables, water, and live animals that would be slaughtered at sea for meat. Many more delays further frustrated the fleet's captain. Sebastian told me the longer we waited, the danger from hurricanes increased. I'd only heard of hurricanes, never experienced one, and he told me it was the worst storm I could imagine.

"I asked other sailors about hurricanes, and they shook their heads and told me to pray to God we never would see one. They said even the most hardened and vile among them would cry out for his soul's salvation in the unimaginable raging storm. I hoped never to experience one, but that was not to be. Little could I realize how one would change my life forever."

# Chapter 6

Roger said to Will, "This is pretty interesting."
Will said, "Keep reading. It gets even more interesting."

"After eight long months of waiting, the Flota was ready to sail. Thirteen ships laden down with treasure, food of all kinds, and people set sail for the perilous two-month voyage to Spain. Sebastian pointed out a particularly beautiful noblewoman, senora Nunes, and her husband as they boarded. He said God blessed the nobleman for having such a fine wife. Our small ship carried almost two hundred souls and was very crowded above and below deck. A French warship, the *Grifon*, reluctantly was forced to join us. France was our ally now, for the time being.

"Sebastian told me our ship was carrying a special cargo, but I was not to repeat this, and he did not specify what this special cargo treasure was. Our small ship was filled with tobacco, so I could not understand what he meant, but I trusted him and asked no questions. We would eat well on the fresh foods in the beginning, fruits and vegetables from Cuba and the live animals to be slaughtered as needed. Then we must subsist on the large quantities of hard biscuits, salted fish and meat, corn, beans, cheeses, oil, and wine. God willing, the water carried in earthenware pots, casks, and six-foot-long sealed segments of bamboo thick as a man's thigh would hold out. A thirsty crew and passengers would be a dangerous combination. It was the job of the water constable, the *alguacil de agua*, to see it lasted to the end. A big and mean man with no sense of humor usually held that job, and ours was no exception.

"We set sail with much fanfare on July the 24th in the early afternoon. The captain and sailors seemed in good spirits as the weather and winds were fair till we reached the point to turn between the narrow straits where Florida and the Bahamas Islands were closest. Here the winds became erratic, and we were forced to tack back and forth but made little progress. Frequently, they died altogether. Also, the lookouts warily watched the horizon for any sign of a strange sail. Privateers and pirates roamed these waters. News of the peace treaty may not have reached these waters, and some may choose to purposely ignore the end of hostilities to capture a final war prize.

"Conditions became worse the next day as we moved north along the coast of Florida. At midday, a strange milky haze fell on us. The blue sea became gray like lead as long, steady swells hit our ship. It creaked and moaned like it was alive. Sailors complained their joints ached, and it was a sure sign of coming bad weather.

"Dawn broke on Tuesday, July 30[th,] humid with a hot oppressive heat. The sun seemed covered with a thin and yellowish gauze. The waves grew ever larger. Soon every man, woman, and child sensed the grave danger ahead. Gray clouds grew to the east and south, and by afternoon, it became so black and dark, the stern lanterns were lighted. Shortly afterward, the storms first mighty blast came staggering the fleet. The captain ordered the men to secure the violently flapping sails, and they did the best they could in the howling winds trying to rip them and the sails off. The bilge pumps were barely able to keep up with the water coming in from the waves and rain that came like arrows. Many gales viciously pounded our ship each one worse than the one before. It was midnight, but no one could sleep. Sailors were washed overboard and lost. The mast and sails came crashing down. Women screamed in horror as trunks, bales, barrels, and livestock washed about in the confusion. We threw all the tobacco overboard. Wet tobacco was not something we needed in this storm. We threw everything else we could spare to lighten our ship. Somehow, we managed to survive the onslaught, but again, conditions became still worse. Every vessel was on its own. In the darkness, we felt our ship's bottom strike something, probably a reef. We could feel a gigantic wave in the sea lift her and carry her far, but to where we did not know. We feared no one would survive in the blackness of this maelstrom. The ship came to rest somewhat intact, but the wind still wailed, and rain pelted anyone who tried to go topside.

"At daybreak, the winds died down, and sailors ventured outside to assess our situation. First light in the ship gave us a glimpse of our condition. Some had survived, but our condition was dire. That was apparent to all lucky enough to live, but many would soon envy the dead, and many still alive would join them. We heard a call for all to come topside. No one was prepared for what we saw. Our ship had no masts. Only one small boat that could hold no more than six remained on the deck. The first mate assembled all before him and spoke, 'We are all that remain. The captain is dead, perished in the storm. We have a little food and water, thank God, but little gunpowder that is not wet and only one gun left. We have survived the storm, but now must survive this hostile land. The best I can figure it out, our ship is aground in the Lost Lagoon, but I know not where on the Florida coast.'"

Roger stopped, "Lost Lagoon? Where's that?"

Will said, "I was curious about that too. I found some notes on the back that seem to me the writer was referring to what we today call the Indian River, but where exactly in it, I don't know. Read some more, and I think it will become clearer."

"Okay," Roger said. He started again. "Today, we will find the dead still on the ship and bury them as best we can. We will make shelters on the deck from what we have. Today, we must organize ourselves and take stock of what and who we have, their abilities, and to their needs. To the east, there seems to be an inlet to the sea. I have heard tales of inlets being cut during storms like this, and I think our ship rode in and through the new channel to where our ship now sits. Tomorrow, I will send men in the small boat that survived to see if that is true and see if others in the twelve ships may be live. Are there any questions?' There were many, but the ones about missing loved ones were the hardest. The first mate confirmed seeing the bodies of some whose names were mentioned, but on others, he did not know. Senora Nunes husband was among the missing. He had gone up to try to help the sailors during the storm and had not returned. I feared the answer she would receive, if she got one, would not be good if she got one at all."

Roger stopped. "It's an interesting tale, but what does this have to do with the emerald and our dead man?"

"Read on," Will said. "You'll soon find out."

# Chapter 7

Roger stopped him. "Why don't you read? You've finished off your beer and I've hardly taken a sip between reading and talking. You've read this already and won't be stumbling over the words like a first-time reader. Besides, we don't want you going back to the shop with loads of brew smells on you."

"True," Will said. "Let me point something else out. In the notes someone made, it mentions storm surge, full moon, high tide all with question marks. Do you know what that means?"

"Not really. Please enlighten me."

"As you may have guessed, it deals with the hurricane. I asked myself; could a ship really get over the barrier island into the Indian River? In many places, the barrier island is very narrow even today."

"And you think one could?" Roger said.

"I do, if conditions were right. New inlets happen after hurricanes, especially in the old days. With the right conditions, the ocean could be maybe, up to sixteen feet above normal. Sometimes, hurricanes produce waves of thirty feet, even fifty is possible."

Roger whistled. "The perfect storm."

"Correct. With those conditions, it could have happened, and I believe it did just as this story says."

"You're the expert on this," Roger said. "My experience with hurricanes has been up north and far inland. We could get some winds, maybe even a tornado, but I never imagined the ocean that high. I've seen what six to nine inches of rain can do to rivers, and it ain't pretty."

"Under those conditions, most of the barrier island could have been underwater. Even low areas on the mainland would have been inundated for a while. I'd hate to see something like that happen today."

"It'd be bad." Roger stopped. "What else do the papers say?"

"Okay. I read. You drink beer," Will said.

"Sounds good to me." Roger took a gulp. "Proceed, young man."

"Okay. 'The survivors picked up on the urgency in the first mate's voice and did what we could in spite of lack of sleep, food, water, and fear of what was ahead. Everything was wet, and many people were half naked because of the storms fury. We settled in for the night we hoped would be peaceful, but it was not to be. Two men stood watch at all times in case Indians showed up. Many believed them to be hostile. That night, no Indians appeared, but mosquitoes fell on us like one of the plagues of ancient Egypt. And then the rains and winds returned. Many said the hurricane had returned to finish us off. The ship rocked back and forth in the river and rain poured in through the cracks. All night long, it harassed us only giving up trying to kill all who had survived its first fury shortly before daybreak. At dawn, everyone, went topside and prayers were said to Mary and the Holy Father for our making it through the night alive. What little food and water we had were rationed out into meager meals, but we were thankful for anything to put in our empty stomachs.

"We set to the task of making temporary shelter on the ship. Men were sent out in the small boat to check to see if somehow we could get our ship back to the sea through the new inlet and to look for any more survivors from the other ships. When they returned, the news brought a new chill to us. The storm during the night had closed the inlet, and they saw only bodies and debris on the beach, no survivors. We were on our own in Palmar De Ays, the land of the Ays Indians. One of the sailors found a crippled dolphin struggling in the water. We ate it for our evening meal.

"Of the original two hundred people on the ship, only 35 had survived by the second day after the shipwreck. Twenty were sailors. Ten were nobles, five of those women, and the remaining 5 were children. Our commander selected five men to take the small boat and row north up the river and see if they could get to St. Augustine and bring help. He picked Sebastian, myself, and three other sailors, one, a rough man named Manuel, who still had a gun that worked and a little dry powder. Senora Nunes begged to go with us. She said having a woman on board might convince the warlike Ays we were peaceful. The commander considered this and granted her request. She would take the place of one sailor, but she must row. She agreed. Whether the commander felt she was correct or thought we were fewer mouths to feed till a possible rescue found the ship, I do not know. Setting out for St. Augustine, somewhere to the north seemed a better alternative than staying put and waiting for something I doubted would ever come. They gave us as much food and water as they could spare, and we set off the next morning at dawn. We managed to rig a small sail that helped us.

"On the second day with the sun high overhead, we saw another boat coming from far away. Indians! We tried to escape, but to no avail. Sebastian told Manual not to fire his gun, but he did anyway. He missed, and this only made the Indians mad. I tried to protect the Lady and Sebastian shouted strange words to the threatening Ays. They killed Manual and the other sailor and grabbed the Lady and me and tied our hands. Only Sebastian was left unbound. I asked him why the Indians we treating us so, and he said he spoke some of their language. He had traded with them on another voyage at another time. He told them the Lady was his woman, and I was his brother. His tale had saved our lives, for now. Sebastian told them he was a friend of their chief, a man named Xarxez. We would be taken to their village, and our fates would be determined there.

"When we arrived there, they stripped us of our tattered clothing that had barely covered us. I tried not to look at the beautiful noble Lady, but found my eyes wandering back to her, though many Indian in the village from children to adults, men and women were naked also. The Lady tried to cover herself but soon gave up the futile attempts. We were brought before the chief, a big and strong man clothed only in beads around his neck. He spoke to Sebastian in his native language, and Sebastian responded in kind. The chief remembered him. They spoke for some time and then braves with knives came to the Lady and me. I feared the worse, but they only cut our binds. We were free. They motioned for us to be seated around a fire and then they gave us some food and water. It was good. For the first moment in some days, I was able to relax and not be afraid. It was about that time I realized I had been aroused by all the naked women. The Indians pointed out my enlarged organ and laughed. I tried to laugh too, but it would be some time before seeing so much flesh became normal, and I was not aroused. I think the name they gave me, Edatyme, was not a compliment, but a reference to my organ I had difficulty with. I asked Sebastian what it meant, but he just smiled and said it was a fitting name for me.

"They showed us a shelter for the night, and we spent it there. Sebastian told us the chief said we could stay and live with them as they do, but to attempt escape was death. The Lady was very fearful at first and clung to Sebastian, but she, like all three of us, slowly adjusted to life with the Ays.

"We talked about leaving, but Sebastian said we should learn their way of survival in this new land. If we did get the chance to leave, we would need these skills. We were treated well by the supposedly hostile Ays. Time went quickly. There was always something to learn or do. After being there four or maybe five moons, it became apparent to all that the Lady was pregnant. I was not surprised. I had been watching the way Sebastian looked at her and she him. The natives did some dance they said was good medicine for the mother and child, but it was not to be. The child survived the birth, but his mother did not. Sebastian was in great distress. After a long talk with the chief, Sebastian presented the child to an Ays woman whose nursing child had died the day before. The white baby quickly took to her brown breasts. 'It is done,' he said in Spanish. 'This child has brought our freedom. He will stay, and we can leave. That was the chief's offer. What else could I do? The child would die without a mother to care for him.' Reluctantly, I agreed. We buried the Lady after the Indians had a ceremony with much crying and weeping.

"We left two days later. We had been with the Ays for over a year and were nearly as brown as them. They gave us a canoe, some food, and pointed us in the direction of our people, the Spanish. We wondered about the people we had left on the ship. It took us a full day to find it. It was burned to the waterline, and no one was around. We found a skull and some bones in the shell of the ship, and chests, some large and some small. What became of those we left, we never found out, but the boxes contained a surprise to me, the Queen's jewels. True to Sebastian's word, our ship, one of the least in the Flota, had been carrying the greatest treasure. We put three chests, one large and two small, in the canoe. They contained coins and some gold and silver jewelry with precious stones inlaid in them. There were also some emeralds. Sebastian said he had never seen any that big. With that, we

32

set off north up the river. After four days of rowing, we reluctantly left the large box on an island. The extra weight was exhausting us. We would return for it later. We rowed for two more days and were very tired. At a small spring on the western shore, we got water and buried one of the small boxes.

"For ten days, we traveled seeing no one. On the eleventh day, we met a man fishing. At first, he thought we were Indians, and tried to escape, but we convinced him we were subjects of the Spanish King and asked for his help. We could not go into town naked. He agreed to get us clothing when we showed him a gold coin. While he was gone, we buried the small box, but kept some coins to use as we became established in St. Augustine. He returned later that day with some items to wear, and we made our way to the town. It was good to be among our own, but the town was depressing. There had been a drought, and everything was scarce. The yearly Flota from Cuba was late to only make matters worse. We were brought before the commander of the stone fort, Castillo de San Marcos, who questioned us. We told him we survived the Flota disaster, but were captured by the Indians, and been forced to live with them. We escaped and made our way here. He seemed satisfied with our answers and said some had been rescued and some of the treasure had been salvaged. Perhaps, we were omens of good fortune.

"The next day, it rained for the first time in a month, and the following day a ship with supplies arrived. It stayed at the port for a week. Sebastian and I went and recovered some more of the treasure we had buried nearby. He had grown tired of this New World and wanted to return to Spain. He would leave on the ship. The treasure, he said he would hide and use it to repurchase a farm or shop or home. 'A woman and children were what he wanted,' he said and begged me to come, but I did not. Thoughts of retrieving the lost treasure we knew of filled my head. I never married or knew the love of a wife or children. In vain, I searched the rest of my life trying to finding it, but never found more than a very little. There was so much. How I wished I had listened to Sebastian and gone back as he did. My friend, take these words from an old man who knows. Do not spend your short life seeking treasures here on earth. Be like Sebastian. I should have known better. Solomon in the Bible said it best, 'Vanity, vanity, all is vanity.' Our lives are like the morning mist that soon disappears. Spend your life loving your God and your family. Heed my words of wisdom. Learn from my mistakes and live, truly live."

Miguel Brazo

"Wow," said Roger. "That was some tale. Do you really believe it's true?"

"I do," Will said. "And I think the emerald is part of the lost treasure. Someone or someones are looking for it, and I don't think they're taking Sebastian's advice."

Roger nodded, "Nor I. I think it's about to hit the fan."

Will sighed deeply. "I think we need to watch our backs."

A loud boom rang out, and both men hit the floor. Roger looked at Will, "What was that?"

"That," he said, "was a truck backfire."

"I think you're right. Sure scared the hell out of me. You ready to get back to work?"

Will said, "I better do that."

"Be careful," Roger said.

"I will."

"Same here. Same here."

# Chapter 8

Roger watched as Will got into the county van. He made a quick turnaround in the rutted road and quickly disappeared.

He rubbed K9's chin and scratched behind her ears. "Good dog. What do you think of all that? You think all that treasure would be a good reason to kill for? I sure do. Seen it happen for far less. Looks like we have a possible motive. Now we need some possible suspects." Roger thought on this for a few moments.

A truck rolled up in front of the trailer. Lester got out, opened the dummy-locked gate, and began to walk toward them. K9 barked. "No K9. I don't think Lester would be a suspect in the case, but he may be guilty of feeding hungry dogs donuts they shouldn't have." She barked again.

"Permission to come on board," shouted Lester.

"Permission granted. Come on in."

Lester made his way into the screened-in porch. "Can I get you something?" Roger asked.

"One of them cold beers sure would be good."

"Coming right up. What brings you here today, Lester?"

"Several things. You in a hurry? Got some time to talk?"

"Sure do. Will, the county coroner, just left. Gave me some info. Let me get you that beer. This one's 'bout done, and I think I need another."

"Okay," Lester said.

Roger got two beers from his refrigerator and gave one to Lester. Both men took a big gulp and sat down. K9 nudged Lester's leg. "Oh, sorry K9, I forgot to give you a donut. Here you go." She swallowed it in 3 quick bites and looked for more. "Sorry old girl. That was my last one. No more. Gone. See?" He held us his empty hands.

K9 looked disappointed and walked away. She lay down on a rug and closed her eyes. Roger said, "Now look what you did. Got her on a sugar high and soon she'll be in lalaland."

Lester smiled, "Yeah. Works every time."

"You know Lester, I think I understand something now I didn't before."

"How's that?"

"I understand some things about myself, and I understand why I feel somewhat of a kinship with Will. Archaeology and crime scene work have a lot in common. You must destroy in order to find what's there. In an archaeological excavation, you gotta dig up the site, see what you find, interpret it, and analyze what you found. A crime scene is similar. In both, you only get one chance to get it right. If you do it wrong, you never get another opportunity because you destroyed what you were trying to solve."

Lester nodded, "Yeah. That do make sense to me."

"So what's on your mind, Lester?"

"You notice your phone is working? I flagged down Ernie the phone guy while you were at the church. I told him it was a favor for Bill, and he got right on it. Bill won't like me callin' in his favors, but he'll get over it. It was storm damage from that electrical storm. Fried some wires. He fixed them so you should be getting calls."

"No. I don't think Bill would like it you using his favors on me. Do it again." The men laughed.

"Lester, I am. I'm getting the usual ones from people trying to sell me something or wanting something, so I had caller ID installed and bought an answering machine so I can screen my calls. It cost a few bucks, but was worth it."

Lester said, "It do, but it's well worth it. I've had both of those for some time. You get calls from people you don't want to talk to, too?"

"Yeah. I got two calls from the county. I recognized it as one in the series of numbers they use, but I didn't realize it was from Hernandez till the third call where she left a message with some foul language in it tell me to return her bleeping call immediately or else."

"So did you?"

"Of course not. Lester, my phones still giving me fits. Don't you know that?" Roger gave a knowing wink to the old black man.

"Oh, I gotcha. Don't you think that will make her more mad?"

Roger smiled. "Yeah, that was my whole intent. I have to establish some ground rules with her. I'm not going to be under her thumb and jump like a puppet on a string for her. I'll call her tomorrow and see what she wants." He paused. "Now, what's on your mind?"

"Like you asked, I did a thorough review of the electric system of this place. It ain't good. It's a wonder it ain't caught fire and burn down with all the contents."

Roger said, "Like that would be a big loss."

Lester said, "But if that happened, K9 might die. And your new cat too."

"What about me? Aren't you concerned about me?"

"No more than you are. Seems wrong for a dumb animal to die, but you should know better. The wiring in this place looks like something Tom Edison's half-wit brother put in. And throw the lightning damage on top of it, it's bad. Really bad."

Roger sighed. "Okay, I get the picture. I'm no electrician. What's it gonna cost to fix it right?"

Lester told him all that needed done and quoted a figure. Roger's eyes grew wide, and he whistled. "That much?" he said.

"That much. I only use quality parts, and I don't cut corners. I stand behind my work."

Some profanity slipped from Roger's lips. "That's high. Higher than I expected, but I do want it fixed right, if not for my sake, I want the animals to be safe."

"I was hoping you'd see it that way. I got some of the emergency parts in my truck, and I can start immediately."

"You do that."

Lester asked, "Money gonna be a problem?"

"Nah. I got it covered. Fact is, I did want to talk to you about money."

"Oh? Why you want to talk to me about money?"

"Bill said you're good with it. I need some advice."

Lester said, "That Bill is a blabbermouth, but I guess he trusts you, so I'll help you with the little I know."

Roger smiled, "I think you know more than you're saying on the matter. Bill told me in confidence you were one of the richest men in the county. Is that true?"

Lester asked, "You ever known Bill to lie?"

Roger laughed. "I have. Is the Pope Catholic?"

Lester smiled, "If Bill said it to you in confidence, it must be true. What do you need to know?"

# Chapter 9

"I got a problem," Roger said. "Actually, I got a lotta problems, but the one I'd like you to help me with is one involving money. I need some advice. Would you help me with that?"

A little smile came to Lester's weathered dark face. "Yeah, I think I can help you with dat. And I might even be willing to help you with some others if you would like."

"Thanks for the offer, Lester, but right now a sympathetic ear and a little direction would be most helpful with my money problem. I own this property outright, which is a good thing. I have no debt, and I've got lots of money in the bank because of a life insurance policy on my late wife and the settlement I got from the university."

Lester nodded. "That sounds good. So what's the problem?"

"The bank ain't payin' me squat in interest. Inflation and taxes are eating the little bit of growth happening. Got any idea how I can really make it grow and take off?"

"Have you thought about mutual funds?"

"No, not really. I can tell you all about bones and civilizations thousands of years old, but I don't know much about mutual funds."

"Well, Roger, just find a good broker and decide how much risk you're willing to take. Big risk means wide swings, possible big gains and loses. Moderate risk gives growth and less ups and downs. Low risk comes with a low chance of growth, but little chance of loss. You got to decide which one is right for you. How much risk you can handle. You got money market, stocks, gold, and savings funds. Whatever you like and whatever risk you want to take. That's the nutshell version."

"Got anyone locally you would recommend, someone you trust?"

Lester said, "Yeah, I do. Go with a credit union financial planner, one on salary. You need to be a member. You a member of one anywhere?"

"None here, but I'm a member of First People's Credit Union back up home. I know the guy there, Eric Stadermann, good and honest fellow."

Lester said, "He might be a good one to start with. Got lots of good credit unions here too. Start small, get comfortable, invest some more, but never more than what you can afford to lose."

"Sounds like some good advice. Need another beer?"

"Nah," Lester said. "I'm still nursing this one. Thanks."

"Lester, I don't really know too much about you. Could you tell me a little about yourself? I'd like to know."

"Well, I'm usually a pretty private person, but since you're a friend of Bill and I think you are going to stay in this little town, I'll tell you some." He cleared his throat. "I was born back in the bad ole days of segregation and Jim Crow. The Klan was active in our area, which didn't have many people back then, about 25,000 souls. Every black family carried a copy of the Green Book with them when they traveled in the South."

Roger said, "Can't say I ever heard of the Green Book. What was its purpose?"

"People like me weren't welcome in a lot of places back then, to put it mildly. A fellow by the name of Green compiled a list of places where we could find a decent place to sleep and get a meal, maybe even a drink, and not be harassed."

"I can't imagine what that must have been like. I can barely remember seeing Whites Only signs growing up. There was only a few like that where I grew up. When we visited relatives in Virginia and North Carolina that was where I saw them. It must have been hell living in those times."

Lester said, "It wasn't always easy, but that was the way it was. Somehow, we made it through. Don't want to go back to those days."

"Did you go to a segregated school around here?"

"They were all segregated back then. My daddy never had much education. He made it to the third grade before he had to go to work to help his family. He always wanted his kids to do better than he did. I didn't take it too serious until an incident when I was in the sixth grade."

Roger said, "I think I'm about to hear a story."

"You are. We had this young teacher fresh out of college, and we liked to push the limit with her. One day in history class, she asked me, 'Who signed the Declaration of Independence?' I said, 'Damned if I know.' She asked again, and I gave her the same response. She was mortified and sent a note home to my father telling him her question, my response, and that I was suspended until I gave a proper answer. To her surprise, my dad showed up with me as her class began the next day. In front of the whole class, he said he had her note from me. He said he didn't have no book larnin' to amount to nothin' nor my maw either, but they was good God fearin' folks and tried to do what was right and wanted me to do the same. He looked at me real serious and said, 'Son, if you signed the damned thing, admits to it. Take your punishment, and let's move on.'"

Roger said, "That must have brought the roof down."

"It did. And I never sassed a teacher again. I started taking my studies serious 'cause I knew my dad was watchin' and schoolin' meant a lot to him."

"I moved up to the all colored Monroe High School in Cocoa. We was the Wildcats, and I played football. I even lettered. Seemed like everything we had there were hand-me-downs from the white schools. I had some good teachers who encouraged me to be all I could be, and I never forgot that. One of the teachers had a little money. I think it came from rum-running from the Bahamas during the Depression, but that was kind of a hush-hush story, and I never asked. He had a plane and started a Civil Air Patrol at our school. He took a bunch of us boys up, and I was hooked. It changed my life. I was the only one of that group that pursued it and learned to fly."

"You learned to fly? I've often wondered what that would be like."

"Flying was great. It got me into the Army Air Force. I was one of the Tuskegee Airmen. I flew a red-tailed P-51. Shot down three Krauts I did. Got a medal for it, too."

"That's interesting."

"Don't get me wrong. It wasn't a fun time, but it helped make me the man I am today. All of our officers were white, and a lot of them didn't like us. I had one by the name of Gleason. He rode me like a rented mule. One day, I caught him alone and was gonna whoop the tar out of him. I didn't care he was a white officer, and I wasn't. I got a few punches in before he decked me. Turned out he was a Golden

Gloves Boxing Champion. When I got my wind, I told him I hated him for how he treated me worse than all the others. He smiled and said some words I'll never forget. He said, "Young man, I saw something in you, something good, but the only way I knew to make you work to be the best and survive this war, was to push you to your limit and beyond what you think you can ever do. I wanted you to succeed and live and go home and make America a better place.

"Roger, I was so shocked you could've knocked me over with a feather. He walked away and never said a word of my actions against him. He rode my black ass even harder after that, but when he did, I just smiled because I understood him. The other black airmen noted my changed attitude and wondered what had gotten into me. They thought I was trying to kill him with kindness. I never told them what had happened. Years later, I tracked him down to where he had a home in northern Alabama. I wanted to thank him for pushing me to develop the potential he saw in me, but it wasn't to be so. His wife showed me his grave. He had died four months before. I put an American flag on his grave and saluted. His wife gave me a hug. A bunch of locals didn't like it, but when she pulled a .32 out of her purse and told them to mind their own business and get the hell outta here or she would send them to the promised land, they left in a big hurry. That old bird was as tough as the old man.

"After the war, I bought property here in Canaveral Flats. That's how I met Bill Kenney, Sr. and then Bill Kenney, Jr. The dream of the man who created this little burg was a place where all people of goodwill were welcome and treated the same. Not everyone in that era thought like that. The Klan showed up at my house one evening at dusk with the intent on burning us out. A couple of shotguns the Kenneys pointed at them, and the gun I got from the NRA changed their minds and probably saved our lives."

Roger said, "I heard some of that story before. Can't remember if you told me or if it was Bill. Tell me, what's your philosophy of life?"

"That's a big question. Will the Cliffs Notes version do?"

"Whatever you care to share."

"Okay," Lester said. "Surround yourself with people of good character. It's better to be alone than in bad company. Nothing ever comes to one that is worth having, except as a result of hard work. I liked many of the sayings of Booker T. Washington."

"Yeah, he grew up in West Virginia near Charleston."

"One and the same. Born into slavery. Son of some white man and a slave woman. Made the best of what he had. Always worked to be a winner and not whine about his start. He worked hard to improve himself and lift others up. He strove to be a victor, not a victim and hated those who made themselves fat parasites by living on the blood of the unfortunate. Those leeches weakened the people they pretended to help. He said, 'There is another class of colored people who make a business of keeping the troubles, the wrongs, and the hardships of the Negro race before the public. Having learned that they are able to make a living out of their troubles, they have grown into the settled habit of advertising their wrongs – partly because they want sympathy and partly because it pays. Some of these people do not want the Negro to lose his grievances, because they don't want to lose their jobs.'"

Roger nodded. "Yeah, I know people like that. They're sometimes called race pimps, but you find them everywhere – some televangelists, politicians, community organizers, and the like. It's sad."

"It is. How I long for the day when we become like Martin Luther King said, 'a color-blind society where people would not be judged by the color of their skin, but by the content of their character.' I heard him speak while I was in Alabama."

"Yeah, I agree. It'll be a great day when we all see each other as just human beings with different color coverings than divided artificially by racial labels."

Lester said, "Yes, just a colorful kaleidoscope of people all made in God's image. I used to get mad at one particular party for their history of support for slavery and segregation, but there are some good people in both parties. Some time ago I got wind that that same bunch that wanted to burn me out had arranged to get some bad dude biker gang to finish the job. I pulled in some favors. I knew some people who knew some people who knew our governor. Now you didn't hear this from me, but he had some contacts in the construction trade. Seems early one morn, two D9 bulldozers drove through the biker's clubhouse while some state cops watched from a discreet distance. They got the message, and that was the last time I had trouble from them."

"That's an incredible story."

"And I deny ever telling it to you, Roger."

"Right. Gotcha. Never happened."

"Now, you want to keep talking, or should I start work on the electrical system of this firetrap?"

"Just one more question and then I'd like you to start the work. Do you know anything about the 1715 Spanish Treasure Fleet that shipwrecked on our coast nearby? And specifically about something commonly called the Queen's Jewels?"

"I know a little, not much. There's a museum over in Cape Canaveral dedicated to it. You may want to start there."

"Thanks, Lester. I'll check into it."

"And Roger..."

"Yes?"

"Be careful. Wherever there's gold, there's greed and some people will kill their own brother for gold."

"I'll remember that part from you, Lester. Think you can get the electrical work done today?"

"I'll do what I can. I'll need to turn the main power off for a while and then some circuits when I work on them. You may not have all of your outlets working tonight."

Roger said, "So what? That will be better than it is now. Just give me some lights to find the bathroom and make sure the refrigerator has power. Got to keep the beer cold."

Lester smiled, "Yeah, with beer, you got to be able to find the bathroom. Mind if I grab another one to sip while I work?"

"Nope, help yourself. Say, do you think that treasure museum in Cape Canaveral would be open today?"

"They're closed on Monday, and it ain't Monday. I think they should be open."

"Well, you work on my electrical problems here, and I'll head over there and gather information. I might even stop in on Hernandez and see what burrs she's got under her saddle and what she wants. She's not too happy with me I hear for some reason. Got any oil I can pour on troubled waters?"

"No. I'd probably give you the wrong oil anyway. I'd give motor oil when you'd need olive oil. You're gonna have to figger this one out on your own."

"I think you're right on that one, Lester. Think I'll leave now. Check on the animals and see they have water and food please."

"Sure thing." Lester watched as Roger drove off. "Well K9, I hope he knows what he's getting himself into, but I doubt it. It smells to me like trouble's a brewing. You know something else K9, your master may not have much luck at the museum. I just remembered they got robbed a day or so ago. They may not be open. I know it was in the paper, but I see Roger ain't been keeping up with reading the paper lately." Lester gazed at 4 or 5 Florida Today papers lying in their thin plastic bags unopened in a corner of the screened porch. "Oh well, guess he'll find that out real soon and deal with it. While he's over there, wonder if he'll stop in on Hernandez? I bet the fur will fly if he does."

# Chapter 10

The trip from Canaveral Flats to Cape Canaveral was a short fifteen-minute drive but eventful for Roger. When he tried to merge onto State Route 528, a Camaro with gold and black New York tags, blasted by him. He swore at the driver and wished him a rotten day. He prayed a little prayer for God to bless him with a cop. Two miles down the road, he saw blue lights flashing. A Cocoa cop, who often sat in the dip just past the Indian River Drive bridge, had the speedster pulled over and seemed to be arguing with the driver. Roger smiled and wished the cop a good day. *Well, God does answer prayers.*

It was one of those hot mornings with next to no air movement. The Indian River had been a sheet of glassy water. The road changed to A1A after a traffic light, and Roger saw the sign directing him to his destination, the Sunken Treasure Museum. He pulled into an empty parking lot which puzzled him. Where was everyone? He walked to the front door and saw a closed sign on it although another sign giving the weekly schedule said the establishment should be open. He saw a bell at a nearby door for deliveries and rang it twice.

After a short wait, the door opened, and a short man with a big gun appeared and demanded, "Who are you, and what do you want?"

Roger stepped back and put his hands up. "Sorry partner if I caught you at a bad time. I'll be leaving now."

"Not till you answer my questions. Who are you, and what do you want? And I'm not your partner."

"Sorry. My name's Roger Pyles, and I'm with the police department. I was hoping you could answer some questions I have."

The short man looked at him closely and said, "The cops were already here. I told them everything I knew. What more do you want?"

"I'm investigating the death of a man found in the Indian River. He had an emerald in his stomach that could be part of the lost 1715 Spanish Treasure Fleet cargo. I'm new to the area, but was told this museum was dedicated to that fleet and I could find information about it here. Is that correct?"

The short man said nothing for a minute, and Roger could see he was thinking about his response. "So, you're not here about the robbery?"

"No."

"What did you say your name was again?"

"Pyles, Roger Pyles."

"You're late. Agent Hernandez said you would be here yesterday. What took you so long?"

Roger's face showed surprise. "Really? My phone's been out of order so looks like I've missed a few things. Can I put my hands down now?"

"Aren't you the guy who's been involved in solving several murders lately?"

"Yeah, that's me."

"Thought so. I remember seeing your picture in the paper. Come on in. Care for a cup of coffee? We can talk about this in my office. It's the first door on the left."

Roger lowered his hands and walked in. The short man locked the door behind him and placed a bar across the door for added security. Roger found the coffee, poured himself a cup, and took a seat in a comfortable chair. The short man came in. His gun was now holstered at his side. "Sorry for pointing the gun at you, Mr. Pyles."

"I'd prefer it if you called me Roger."

"Okay, Roger it is. So, you're not here about the robbery, but something else?"

"I came over about the dead man with the emerald in his stomach, but looks like I need to get information on what happened here too." Roger noted the short man was looking at him strangely. "Pardon me, sir," Roger said, "but I didn't catch your name."

The man sighed, "Sorry, I've had a lot on my mind since the robbery. And little sleep. I'm Skip Wagner. This museum was my idea."

"Lot of Wagoners in the area I came from," Roger said.

"Yeah," Skip said. "It's a very common name with a lot of different ways to spell it. I started a salvage company called Real 8. It was my dream to put our findings here on display. We could make some money from tourists coming to this area of Florida and also use it as a learning center and sales center for items we chose to sell. It was working pretty good till the break-in. They about cleaned us out of everything of value here. We thought we were covered. We had armed guards and a great security system."

"So, what happened?"

"Someone ran our night guard off the road that night. He's still in the hospital. The guard on duty was left for dead. I think they slipped up there, but I believe they meant to kill him. And the thieves drove a stolen truck right through a set of double doors on the side. They were professionals all right and ruthless, but even professionals can and do make mistakes."

"They do. That's how they get caught," Roger said, "Now I understand why you're so jittery."

"They missed a few things of great value, and I've been afraid they'd come back and finish the job." He gave Roger another strange look.

"What?" asked Roger.

"Has anyone ever told you that you look like Sam Elliott?"

"Yup. Happens on a quite regular basis."

Skip said, "You even sound like him."

"Guess I do. I'm waiting for the day when I hear from him, and he tells me someone had come up to him and asked him if he was Roger Pyles."

"That would be funny. I haven't had anything to laugh about for several days. You want to look around at the damage they did? The other cops were here and looked around for evidence. Feel free to ask me questions about the break-in, the Spanish Fleet that went down in 1715 or any Florida shipwreck for that matter, and of course, the green emerald you mentioned."

"Okay, show me around."

"Follow me," Skip said.

Roger did as he was told and followed Skip down a hallway to an area that was covered in unpainted plywood. It had been tap-conned to a block exterior door. Roger said, "I'm not a rocket scientist, but I'd bet this is where they got it."

"Right you are. They drove a stolen truck through the door. The cops are looking for prints now, but I'm not betting on them finding any. This bunch was too good to make mistakes like that."

"Why do you say that?"

Skip said, "After taking out our night shift on the highway, they cut or disabled all electric lines going to this building. No calls in or out and the security battery backup didn't work. Seems there was a power surge last week and the new batteries haven't arrived yet, though there isn't much left to steal.'

"Did you have a power surge from lightning?"

"No. Florida Power and Light checked into it and found evidence of tampering. Someone who knew what they were doing created a surge that effectively fried the circuits our security was on and a few others. It wasn't natural. That's how they got in."

"What about the guard on duty?" Roger asked.

"He'd been drugged heavily. Cops are still trying to figure out how. He's lucky he's not dead. The police took everything they thought could have been used in the burglary for analysis."

"Yeah, dead witnesses don't talk. Did he see anything at all?"

"No. Zilch. Can't remember what happened."

"Do the bad guys know what shape he's in or where he is?"

Skip said, "I doubt it, but the paper reported the guard on duty was alive."

"That'll give them a little to think about. Loose ends, slip-ups aren't something they want."

"Roger, you can look all over this place, but I don't know what more you'll see or find. They cleaned us out. What we had here was worth millions."

"Do you have more somewhere like in a warehouse?"

"This was our warehouse. We had it all in one place with security all around. What more could we have done?"

"I don't know. Hindsight is always 20/20, but that doesn't do us any good at this point. Tell you what. Let me mosey around and see what I can find. A new set of eyes may see something."

Skip said, "Sure. Knock yourself out. I could use some good luck today."

Roger thought of the Camaro and the cop and smiled. "My lucks been good so far today. Maybe I'll find something helpful."

"Take all the time you want. I'm not going anywhere, but I will need to let you out when you're ready."

"Okay, thanks."

Skip said, "I need to make a pit stop. Nature calls. I could be busy if you need me."

Roger said, "Hmm, whatever I find new, if anything, can wait. Don't wanna disturb you when you're taking care of business."

"Thanks. I'll be in my office. Looks like I've got some paperwork to fight with. I'm not holding my breath on getting money out of the insurance company."

"Yup," Roger said. "In the bathroom and office."

"Ain't that the truth?" Skip quickly disappeared around a corner. Roger looked around the boarded-up door for clues, but noticed nothing that would help him. In the next hour, he walked around the museum. It was hard to tell what the crooks had damaged from what the cops had trampled. A few anomalies stuck in his mind, but they could be something or nothing. He had a lot to review, and he needed to see what Agent Hernandez and the rest of the cops had for evidence. He doubted she would be thrilled to see him, but he might as well get the unpleasant over. She wouldn't bite his head off he hoped, even if she wanted to. He wasn't about to lay down and be roadkill either.

# Chapter 11

Roger found Skip Wagner filling out forms at his desk and muttering under his breath. His gun lay on the desk. Skip asked him if he'd found anything of interest or suspicious. Roger said yes, but he needed to talk to Agent Hernandez before saying more. Skip said he understood. Both knew the other's thought. Often the closest to the crime could be the ones who did it. Skip didn't seem too concerned about this. The innocent usually know they are, and it shows. Roger would talk to Hernandez and make sure what he saw was true and ask about an alibi for Skip.

After Skip let him out, he went to his truck. Heat pounded the door, and the steering wheel was almost too hot to handle. He rolled the other window down and started the engine. More heat poured from the vents. It would take a few moments before the air conditioning kicked in. He had the feeling he was being watched but saw nothing out of the ordinary except for the closed museum that should be getting busy at this time of day.

He took a left on A1A which quickly became State Route 528. At Courtenay Parkway, he got off the four-lane expressway, took a left at the light, and then another quick right into the Brevard County Sheriff's Department parking lot on Merritt Island. Luck was with him in he found a spot up close and under a shade tree. Roger had noticed how shade trees in parking lots seemed to draw cars in this sunny state.

The heat hit him again as he walked to the building. Once inside, he saw Charlotte at the reception desk. "Well, hello, Miss Charlotte. How's it goin'? I've not seen you in a while."

"It's goin' good," she said, "and it will soon be Mrs. Charlotte." She held up her hand and showed a new diamond ring.

"Well, congratulations, young lady. Do I know the lucky man?"

"Thanks for asking, but I don't know how you would. His name's Cyrus. He was named after that fella in the Bible. We went to high school together and were sweethearts. We had a falling out over something stupid, you know, teenage stuff and went separate ways. He went into the service, got married and divorced in quick order, got out, came back here, looked me up, and the rest is history. It's like old times, only better." She waved her ring about.

"That's super. I'm glad to see things are going well for you."

She smiled, "Got a raise too out of this stingy county. Now that's a real miracle."

Roger laughed. "I'm here to see Hernandez. Is she in?"

Her face fell. "Yes, she's in, but she's in a foul mood about a bunch of stuff, and your name was mentioned too."

"I thought that might be the case. Could you call her and tell her I'm here and wanting to talk with her?"

Charlotte said, "It's your butt to get chewed, not mine. As I said, she's been awful grouchy lately."

Charlotte made a quick call and soon told him she could see him now. After she put down the receiver, she said, "Be careful. Don't say I didn't warn you."

"I'll be careful. I've dealt with some ornery cusses in my life."

She shook her head. "She can be a real bear at times. For your information, I've been asked so many times on her mood; we now have an early warning system. If you see a sunny Florida picture on my desk, she's sunny. A neutral picture means a neutral mood. If it's a stormy scene, watch out. You've been warned."

"Thanks," he said. "I'll remember that. I see it's the stormy picture today."

"Yeah, category 1 hurricane. Brace yourself."

"Roger that," Roger said. "I always like to say that." He stopped. "Guess I'll get some practice on how to win friends and influence people. Be a regular Dale Carnegie."

"Good luck with that. You're gonna need it," she said.

He smiled, nodded his head, and proceeded up the stairs to her office. Her door was open, so he poked his head in. Agent Hernandez looked up from the paperwork she was busy with. "Take a seat," she said. "I'll be with you in a moment."

"Mind if I get a cup of coffee?"

"No," she grunted. "I've been living on it lately."

Roger got the coffee and sat down. He studied the young woman in front of him. She looked tired, somewhat haggard, and older than he remembered. Stress can do that to you. He sipped at the coffee and tried to read her mood better. She seemed somewhat agitated, but not as bad as he had expected. She set the pen down, put the papers in a folder, and said to him, "Roger Pyles. You're a hard man to get ahold of. I've been thinking about you, and here you are right in front of me."

Roger tried to hide his surprise and for the most part did so. He'd been expecting to be hit with gust force winds or more. "Yes, that information made its way to me by the grapevine. It's better to be a little late in this world, than a little early in the next. My phone's been out of order since the big storm, and I recently discovered it. Seems I've missed some developments."

"That's an understatement if I ever heard one."

Roger said, "This may not be the best time, but there's a bone I need to pick with you."

Her look told him she wanted to talk candid with him, but the look also said she was holding back. "Okay, you first. What's on your mind?"

"I'm wondering how I fit into this organization. What's my official status with the county? What are my duties and responsibilities?"

"Hell if I know," she said. "That's part of my frustration. I've been trying to make some order out of the chaos I found here, and it's like herding cats. Not only am I doing cold cases, but they've got me working fresh ones. I feel like a one-legged man at an ass-kicking contest."

"Sounds like an expression I would have heard up north."

She shrugged. "Picked it up from my dad. Guess he got it from some Yankee living in south Florida. Anyway, about your status, it's complicated, but this is the best explanation I can give you. The county legal department gave me this wheezy answer. As long as you meet the requirements of the town of Canaveral Flats, they're good with you helping."

"Canaveral Flats has no procedure or requirements."

"So I've been told."

Roger said, "The only thing that's been done is this; I was verbally sworn into that one man police force by Bill Kenney in a rinky-dink Mickey Mouse ceremony."

"So I've been told. The county says it will go with whatever the city Canaveral Flats requires of its officers. So the bottom line is, you officially answer to them and not me. I would like to have your help. I need more help. I'd been trying to get you in here because I thought you were working for me, but officially the legal people on the payroll tell me you're with the town, not the county, but there is the mutual assistance provision that all the law enforcement agencies in the county have."

Roger was beginning to understand why she was treating him with kid gloves. It could have all been this jurisdictional point, but there seemed to be something more.

She said, "Roger, I'm not the easiest person to work for. I get frustrated often and sometimes the old pressure relief valve in me kicks in and it ain't pretty. I need your help. The country needs your expertise. I'm asking you to take a more active role in police work here, please."

This was going much better than Roger had ever imagined. He liked the idea, but attempted not to show it though his eyes gave him away. "So the county is good with it as it is now?"

"They are. You're covered by Canaveral Flats rules, and that's good with the county. It covers their backside, so they're happy."

"And the various towns, cities, and the sheriff's department all do have that mutual assistance agreement. So that will keep it all hunky-dory?"

She said, "For now. They're happy so let's leave sleeping dogs lie at this time."

Roger said, "That will work for me. Now that we've got that sticky point out of the way, what did you need to talk with me about?"

She paused and seemed to need a moment to organize her thoughts. "Several things."

# Chapter 12

Agent Hernandez asked, "So, what're you up to now?"

"Gathering information on a case and it may be related to another. You know about the dead man they found in the Indian River?" Roger said.

"Which one?"

"The one up behind the church near Port St. John. The one where the guy was missing an arm?"

"Oh yeah. That one. Been so many lately. With the river being a mile or more wide and about 70 miles long, that covers a lot of territory. That one. What have you got?"

"I helped in the recovery of the body with Bill Kenney and the coroner. It was nasty. Been in the water for some time. I talked with the coroner after he did the autopsy. It definitely looks like a murder and he found a big emerald in the dead man's stomach. He seems to think it may have something to do with a Spanish treasure lost in the area centuries ago. The coroner believed the stone to be part of the Queen's Jewels, a part of the treasure still missing and said to be priceless. I went over to the treasure museum in Cape Canaveral and was greeted with a menacing man with a gun, fellow named Skip Wagner. Said he was the owner and the place had been robbed of most everything of value."

"Roger, try around $750,000 best we can figure. It's the largest robbery of its kind ever to happen in the county."

"Wow. No wonder he was angry. It was insured, right?"

"We'll see. I think he had some insurance, but I don't know if it was enough or if it was the right kind. And with claims this big, the companies have a way of balking on payments. He needs some luck and a good lawyer. I don't think he'll see any kind of a payment for years if he ever does. The lawyers are the ones who'll make out on this."

"Don't they always?"

"True," she said, "but if you listened to them, they're just doing their jobs. Keeping the customer satisfied." She laughed. "About like a stripper leading a drunk on. Take his money and give him just enough to keep the money flowing."

She continued, "Whoever did the robbery were professionals. It was too slick and well thought out. Somebody went to great lengths to pull this massive heist off."

"Any ideas who might have done it? Do you have any suspects?"

"I'm looking into it. The list of bad actors capable of pulling something of this magnitude off isn't that long. This much I can say for sure – we need to be careful. These people are dangerous, and killing those who get in their way is a normal part of how they operate. Watch yourself, Roger. I wouldn't want to see something bad happen to you."

"It's that serious?'

She nodded. "It is."

The surprised look slowly fell from Roger's face. "It's nice to know someone cares about my well-being. I'm just a little surprised it's you."

Her eyes narrowed. "Roger, contrary to what you may have heard, I do have a heart, though, at times, it may be Grinch size. I'm under a lot of pressure, and sometimes I don't handle it well. I don't want anything bad to happen to those around me. And for your information, I know about the pictures on Charlotte's desk, but don't tell her. I look at the pictures to see how others see me. Call it feedback. You can tell her she can tone it down to the mixed weather picture, but please don't tell her I know. She doesn't need to know. Let's keep it a secret."

"Okay, can I have a copy of the report on the robbery?"

"Sure," she said. "I was expecting you'd show up sooner or later."

Roger cringed a little

She acted like she hadn't noticed. "Got one for you." She handed him a copy she had ready.

"Thanks. I'll look this over with a fine-toothed comb and see if anything jumps out at me."

"Do that and keep me informed of any developments or ideas you have. And please answer your phone."

"Will do as long as it stays working. God only knows how long that will be."

She laughed, "So, I'll say a little prayer for you and your phone."

"Sure won't hurt. Hey, don't forget my cat too."

"You have a cat? Still got your dog K9?"

Roger said, "I do. I'm getting to be semi-domesticated again, I guess."

"What next, Roger? A girlfriend or a wife?" His face fell when she mentioned his wife.

"Sorry," she said. "Looks like I hit a tender spot."

Roger nodded, and his face showed pain. "You did." He sighed deeply. "I still miss her and my son. It doesn't hurt as much as it did, but it still hurts. There are days when it feels like the accident that took their lives just happened yesterday even if it was more than two years ago. It's gotten a little bit better, but I don't know if I'll ever be completely over it. There are times…"

"Roger, it's okay to grieve and remember. It's part of being human. God help the man who can't feel pain. He can't feel joy either."

"I think I want to go. Think my business is done here. I'll keep in touch." He rose quickly and left her sitting at her chair.

She wondered. Had she pushed him too hard? Had she stepped into a forbidden area? How should she proceed in the sensitive subject she knew he needed to see and deal with? Life, like police work, was often a series of questions looking for answers that often lead to more questions. She'd have to play it by ear and improvise just like in her job.

\*\*\*

Roger darted down the stairs and past Charlotte in a sprint.

"How was the….." she asked to his departing backside. She shrugged and said to herself, "Not so good, I see," and went back to work.

\*\*\*

Roger opened the door to his vehicle and threw himself inside. How his heart wept. Just when he thought he was making progress, moving on, and getting over it, something like this happens and the wound in his heart was laid raw and wide open again. Oh, how he wanted a drink.

# Chapter 13

"Hello?"

"Is this Chief of Police Bill Kenney?"

"Who wants to know?"

"Chief, this is Big Red."

Bill grunted to himself. *Big Red. How did he get this number and what did he want. This couldn't be good.*

"Chief, Roger Pyles gave me your number."

*I'm gonna kill that Roger when I see him. This can't be good.* "What do you want Red?"

"I think you know I'm the bouncer at the William's Point Tavern."

"I heard."

"Well, your buddy Roger is down here drunk as a skunk and making a nuisance of himself. He's been down here since this afternoon getting loaded and now he's getting to be an obnoxious drunk. He's in no condition to walk let alone drive. I'd throw his sorry ass out and let the chips fall where they may, but seeing how he's a friend of yours, I'm trying to work something out. He got belligerent with me, took a couple of swings, and I threw him into a corner. It's wasn't that hard as drunk as he was. I tried to talk some sense into him. He said he was feeling lower than a snake's navel. He got to talking about losing his wife and kid and how he felt like dying. I think he was tryin' to drink his sorrows away today. He's a mess."

Bill could hardly believe what he was hearing. "Why are you doing this? Why are you telling me this?"

Big Red said, "Chief, I know we have a history. I ain't mad at you for arresting me all those times I was drunk. Hell, if I ever wanted to be arrested, I'd want it to be you. You was just doin' your job, and I had it coming."

"I did hear you had turned over a new leaf, Red."

"I have. I'm making a new start. Got a good job with the Laborer's Union. I'm keepin' order here at the bar and me and my girlfriend are talkin' about maybe getting' married."

"That's all well and good Red, but what's that got to do with Roger?"

"He needs somebody right now, and I hear you're about the closest thing to a friend he has in the world. I know he's been helping you with some police work and I'd hate to see him screw things up and get hauled off to jail or worst. We need to get him outta the bar and home before he hurts himself or someone else, comprende amigo?"

Bill shook his head. Yes, he understood. Roger was on a bender and heading for trouble if there wasn't some early intervention. "Can you keep him under wraps till I get there?"

"That shouldn't be a problem. He looks like he's about to pass out. If he tries to fight me again, I'm puttin' his lights out."

"Can't blame you on that, but hit him in the chin, not the nose. No point breaking it and having blood everywhere."

Big Red said, "Okay. Good suggestion. I'll do that if I need to."

"I'll be there shortly. Thanks for the call. Bye."

"Okay, see ya shortly."

The phone clicked, and Bill heard a dial tone. *Well, what about that? Big Red may really be going legit and cleaning up his act. And Roger was falling down drunk and needed help again.* He sighed. *Better go get him.*

***

Bill pulled his truck into the bar parking lot and saw Big Red outside with Roger slumped in a cheap plastic chair. Red motioned him over, and Bill pulled close. He got out of the truck and walked up to the men. Bill said, "He looks horrible. Did you punch him?"

"No, he did it to himself. Tripped over his own feet and fell."

"He looks bad."

"You should smell his breath. Kill a buzzard he could with it. Let's load him up in your truck. I can ride along and see he stays docile. Nothin' worst than a belligerent drunk wakin' up when you're traveling down US 1."

"That's true, but I don't think you need to know where I live. I can handle him."

Big Red said, "Now Bill, I know there's been trouble between us, but like I said, that's in the past. You need help with this sorry mass of humanity. How about trusting me on this, okay?"

Bill could see Red was smiling in the light from a street light. He was right about needing help with Roger. He thought for a moment. "Okay."

Big Red's smile got bigger. "You won't regret this."

*I hope not.*

They loaded the drunk into the truck and put him in the middle. About half a mile down the four-lane highway, Roger woke up in an animated and foul mood. Big Red popped him in the chin and Roger slumped unconscious. He looked at Bill who said, "He had it coming."

"Glad you weren't mad about that."

"Mad? I've wanted to hit him at times too. Knock some sense in his head. Poor guy's been through a lot, but he needs to start moving on or it'll kill him. I've seen it happen before."

"You're right about that. I seen men waller in their misery, and it took 'em to an early grave."

"It can do that," Bill said.

The two men said nothing more as they drove down US 1. Bill turned on Canaveral Flats Boulevard. Before long, Miller's Store came into view and disappeared. He passed numerous shacks and trailers before he turned on Tangelo Street. After passing several vacant lots, Bill took a left and parked in front of his house.

"This is it. Can you get him to the door while I make the place drunk-proof?"

"Sure. I can handle it."

Big Red got Roger to the door where Bill grabbed him and helped Red with the unsteady man. They tried to lay him on the couch, but he flopped down like a dead fish. They made no effort to move him to a more comfortable position. "Glad that's done," Red said.

"Me too," said Bill. "How you gonna get back to the bar? I need to keep an eye on Mr. Two Sheets in the Wind."

"Well, how about I call my girlfriend to come get me? She won't complain when she hears I was helping out the law and a local man in distress."

"That'll work. Do it," and Big Red did.

Bill could hear the conversation. She said she'd be there in ten or fifteen minutes. Bill hoped she could find the place in the dark with Big Red's directions. He said goodbye to her and then took a seat across from Bill. He said, "I need to talk with you, Chief. It's important."

"What's it about?"

"I hear things," he said flatly.

Bill raised an eyebrow. "You hear things?"

"Yeah, I hear things."

There was a silence for a moment. "What do you hear, Red?"

"I heard some voices, and I think you'll want to know what they said."

"Voices in your head?"

"Yeah, that's where my ears are. I was at work over at the Cape. I'm on one of those new rocket launch towers. It was lunchtime, and I found a quiet place around a corner. I thought I was the only one around until I heard the voices."

"Real voices? Not voices in your head?"

Big Red said, "Yeah, real voices of real people. Not crazy voices that tell you to do bad things. Is that what you thought?"

"You had me wondering."

"Sorry about that. It was two men, I think. Their voices was carryin' through an open pipe that came from somewhere below. I never got a look at them and don't know who they were, but they said something about a dead body found in the river and more."

"So, that did they say?"

For the next five minutes, they went over what Big Red had heard, and Bill was interested.

# Chapter 14

*Where am I? This place looks familiar.* Through his one barely open bloodshot eye, Roger looked around. He was alive, but oh, how his head hurt. He had to be alive. Death wouldn't hurt this bad. Not only did he have a splitting headache, but his chin felt like a horse had kicked it.

No wonder he recognized this place. He was at Bill's house. How did he get here? He needed to know, but he wasn't sure he wanted to know. Probably bad news.

He found his way to the bathroom and nearly fell when he caught his foot on the small threshold. Fortunately, he recovered in time and took care of business. An extremely full bladder reminded him of what he had been doing last night, drinking copious amounts of all kinds of alcoholic beverages. He stumbled out of the bathroom and smelled coffee.

*Coffee! The elixir of life!* He had to find it. He followed the aroma to the kitchen. A red glow from a small light told him where the desired beverage was. He got a cup from the cupboard and filled it full. *Ah, it was good.* After half a cup, he felt a little better. This would work for him for the hair of the dog that bit him.

He heard a noise coming from the back of the house, Bill's bedroom and soon Bill appeared. He was wearing a T-shirt and boxers. His hair was in his face, and he said to Roger, "Well, why don't you make yourself at home? Have some coffee. Donuts are in the white Krispy Kreme box over there."

"Okay, thanks," was all Roger could muster.

Bill got himself a cup of coffee and two donuts. One he gave to Roger.

"Thanks," Roger said.

"Don't mention it."

The two men sat sipping their drink and nibbling on the donuts, but neither said anything for some time. Roger needed some answers, and he could tell Bill was not going to give him any without him asking. Roger asked, "What am I doing here?"

"Good question. What are you doing here?"

Roger said, "I was hoping you could fill in some of the blanks."

Bill gave Roger a dirty look. "Would you believe a guy who looks a lot like Sam Elliott got wasted at a local bar, decided to streak up and down US 1 showing his shortcomings, was hogtied by a bouncer, thrown buck naked into the back of a UPS truck, and delivered to my front door?"

"Last time I streaked was in college with a whole bunch of other crazies."

"Till last night," Bill said and he let that sink in.

"How'd I get dressed like this?"

"You can thank me. I couldn't have a sight like that in my house."

Roger said nothing for a long while. "These look like my clothes."

"They are." Bill could see the wheels were slowly spinning in Roger's foggy mind.

Roger asked, "Did I actually do some streakin' down on the four-lane?"

"No."

Without much conviction, Roger said, "Didn't think so. Is any of what you told me true?"

"About half of it."

"I was afraid so." He stopped. "Which half?"

"Okay, you did get very drunk at the bar, Big Red kept you from making a complete fool of yourself and very possibly ending up in jail, and I did retrieve your sorry wasted body from the bar, and took you to my house where you spent the night on my couch."

Roger stared at Bill for a moment as he digested Bill's statement. "Thanks."

Bill gave him a dirty look. "You're welcome, ole buddy."

"My chin hurts."

"You fell down."

"It feels like Big Red hit me."

"If Big Red had hit you, you'd have a broken jaw."

64

Roger rubbed his chin. "Yeah, guess I would."

Bill shook his head, "You know, you're two hundred pounds of dysfunction."

"I am not," he said sheepishly. "I only weigh one ninety-five." Roger seemed to be pondering something to add to defend himself, but the only thing that came out of his mouth was, "What's for breakfast?"

"Corn flakes."

"Corn flakes. Just corn flakes?"

"With milk, of course. I may have some dried fruit," Bill said.

Roger reached for his wallet and was happy to see he hadn't lost it during the previous night's activities and he still had a $20 in it. "Is my vehicle in the bar parking lot?"

"It should be. I don't think they had it towed. I think your guardian angel Big Red saw they left it. I wouldn't leave it long. The bar owners may change their mind."

Roger said, "I thought as much. Tell you what. You take us over to Umpa's and breakfast is on me. After that, you drop me at the bar, and I'll get my car. Sound like a plan?"

"It does. Give me a moment to get properly dressed, and we can go immediately."

"Good. This ain't no fifteen-minute warning, is it? My wife would tell me she was ready to go, and when I heard that I knew I had fifteen minutes usually."

Bill chucked, "Yup, that sounds like marriage. No, I'll be ready to go as soon as I get dressed."

"Okay, then." Roger took another sip of his coffee. "I'm hungry. Liquid diets don't stick to your innards."

Bill got up. "It won't be a minute," and it wasn't.

The boys were out the door and shortly traveling north on US 1. They saw Roger's vehicle in front of the bar as they drove by. A minute or two later, they pulled into the parking lot of Umpa's Restaurant, but the sign outside now read Jimmies Restaurant. They walked inside, and a woman directed them to a seat, gave them menus, and brought the coffee they asked for. Another woman with an order pad in her hand came.

"Well, hello, Sugar Plum. How long have you been working here and what with the new name of this joint? Everything's the same inside. What's going on?"

"Bill, first off, I took a part-time job here. I wasn't getting enough hours at Lone Cabbage Fish Camp, and I got kids to see are fed and clothed. You know the story."

"I do all too well. Seems all too common. What's with the name change? Marsha's family didn't sell out, did they?"

"Nothin' like that. She just got tired of explaining what an Umpa was and decided to change the name of the restaurant to Jimmies, which was her dad's name. And as you see, not much else has changed. We have a few new chairs to replace some that were getting worn, but it's the same old good American county cookin' you've come to know and love." She looked at Roger, smiled, and asked Bill, "Who's your friend?"

"Roger. Roger Pyles. You met him when we ate at the Fish Camp."

She said, "I thought he looked familiar. I think I seen his picture in the paper. Helped you guys solve some local crimes."

Bill said, "That would be him, and he's buyin' today. Give the bill to him when we're done." Bill looked at Roger. "What're you havin'?"

"Jimmies Big Breakfast sounds appealing." He looked at Sugar Plum. "Get me one of those. I'm starving."

"You better be," she said. "Bill, what'll you have?"

"Get me one of the same. It's not every day Mr. Cheapskate buys."

"Hey," Roger said. "I'm listenin'. I'm not a piece of chopped liver."

Bill grinned, "I know."

Sugar Plum snickered. "I think it's my cue to leave and put the order in. If you guys wanna fight, take it outside, okay?"

Roger said, "Okay. Hey, where's Marsha? I don't see her around."

Sugar Plum replied, "Her day off."

"Bummer," Roger said. "I hoped to see her."

"She'll be in tomorrow. You guys need anything more besides a referee?"

"No," they said in unison.

"Good." She left and gave the cook the order.

Roger said, "Thanks, old buddy. Just about the time I've got enough coffee in me to make me feel half-human again, you kick me when I'm down."

Bill said, "You need kicked, kicked hard. This is my Dutch Uncle Joe speech. Roger, you got to quit drowning your pain with all that alcohol. You need purpose and a reason to go on. You need meaning to your existence. Roger, let me tell you a story. I met a young woman who was on vacation some time ago. She was a Hungarian Jew. She and her family were rounded up by the Nazis. Dr. Joseph Mengele personally separated her from her mother at the train station when the cattle cars carrying the Jews to the concentration camps arrived. He lied to her telling the young girl her mother was going to the showers. Instead, her mother was gassed to death like tens of thousands. The mother's last words were, 'Just remember, no one can take away from you what you put in your mind.'

"Later, Mengele stopped at the prisoner barracks and wanted to be entertained. Because Eva was a ballerina, she was 'volunteered.' A prison band played the Blue Danube Waltz while she danced for one of the worst war criminals the world has ever known. She pretended she was at the Budapest opera house and she danced her heart out. He was pleased and rewarded her with an extra loaf of bread, which she later shared with the other girls in her prison quarters."

Roger said, "Nazis. I wish you hadn't mentioned Nazis."

Bill said, "Yeah, something going on just doesn't smell right, and it could be them."

He continued. "Months later the group was forced to march across Austria in the winter. Anyone who could not keep up was put to death immediately. Eva was sick from disease and starvation and was wavering. The same girls she had helped with the extra rations rescued her and held her up when her strength was gone.

"Later on, she came to America and became a clinical psychologist dealing with people whose life had broken; victims of crime, war, and all kinds of abuse and loss. I still remember what she said, 'Auschwitz, believe it or not, gave me a tremendous gift in some way. I now know first-hand how to guide people to have resilience and perseverance.'

"She said, 'Self-love is self-care. The biggest and meanest concentration camp that exists is in our own minds.'"

"Sounds like someone I'd like to meet and talk to."

"Roger, you may get the chance. She now lives in the area. Roger, you have a choice – be a survivor or a victim. Ever read any Ernest Hemingway?"

"A little."

"I've read several of his novels. I just finished *To Have and Have Not*. Very depressing and gloomy. I think it showed his outlook on life. It's no wonder he blew his head off with a shotgun. No hope. No one cared if he lived or died. That's my opinion. The two world views are so different – survivor or victim of circumstances. It's a choice we all must make."

Roger nodded. "So what keeps you going, Bill? It'd seem to me you must get down sometimes. I mean, every day you face the same problems. Don't seem like nothin' changes. What do you have to show for your efforts? What progress are you makin' to improve your little Podunk corner of the world? I wanna hear it from you."

Bill sighed, "Good question. You know, it does get me down sometimes, but I ask myself what this world would be like if the thin blue line wasn't there to try to hold back the flood. What kind of a world would it be then? I think we have this in common; we both believe in justice, and without people like us, bad guys and gals would be running hog wild, and there'd be no justice. King Solomon in the Bible talked about it in Ecclesiastes. 'What has been will be again; what has been done will be done again.' He complained about the endless, even meaningless cycles of daily human life. I know I can't change the whole world, but I try to make a difference for good in my little, as you called it, Podunk part of the world. You never know when something you do, like show some heartfelt concern and even a little intervention in the daily grind, will meet someone's need, large or small, seen or unseen. That's my purpose. I've been surprised how some situations I had to deal with worked out in the long run. I remember a car wreck on US 1 I was called to. A young woman EMT helped out a young man who was injured. He got her name and when he recovered, tracked her down to thank her. They got to dating and now five years later are married and have two daughters. He said her kindness was what had attracted him to her. You never know how something you do will affect this world. That's my armchair shrink advice, and it's worth every penny you paid for it or more."

Roger nodded. "Thanks. Now, what's this important info you have?"

At that time, Sugar Plum appeared with two big plates full of food. "Here it is boys. I'll get the grits that come with it. And it looks like you need more coffee." She set the plates down and left quickly.

Roger said, "How 'bout we talk about that after we eat? I'm famished, and the smell of this is killing me. My stomach's trying to chew the meat off my backbone."

"I was about to say the same. It can wait till we're done. I don't think a short delay will get anyone killed, but you never know. I hope not."

# Chapter 15

"That was some pretty good grub, Bill. This seems your usual way of cooking – eatin' out, carry-in, or some kind of prepared food you open up."

"Roger, you cut me to the quick with your comments. And you know me too well. It's just me I usually have to worry about, but remember, this was your idea and a good one, for a change, I might add."

"Yeah, I guess it was and one you were all too eager to hop on, Bill."

Bill said, "In all fairness, I do try to get as much fresh fruit and greens in my diet as I can. Seems things have a way of going bad with just me to eat up the whole package."

"That's true."

"But it does keep me a regular guy."

Roger said, "Yeah, I've heard guys that ain't regular get to be grumpy old men."

"And you'd know from first-hand experience I'm sure."

"Guess I'm busted on that one, but I hoped you wouldn't go there. Guess I should have known better."

Bill nodded. "Yes, you should. Now are you gonna discuss our digestive processes or are we gonna talk business?"

"Okay, the food was good, and it was the best idea I've had in some hours. What was the big information you wanted to tell me?"

"I had a nice little talk with Big Red while you were out cold last night."

"And?"

"I got enough material to blackmail you for life if I wanted to."

"Seriously?"

"No," Bill said, "but for all you're worth and more."

"I was afraid of that."

"Seriously, ole buddy. You just got drunk and made an obnoxious idiot of yourself, but who's keeping score." Bill let that sink in. "Seriously, if you go back to that bar anytime soon, you may want to go to an out of the way booth and drink as quietly as a church mouse."

"Didn't know church mice drank."

"Only the Episcopalians and Catholics will admit to it. Not the Baptists."

"Glad you straightened me out on that. Come on. What's the big scoop you've got for me?"

"Just that Big Red overheard some guys on his job site talking about the dead body found in the river behind the church. They seemed to know more than they should have about it, but unfortunately, he didn't see who was talking. The voices were carrying through a large pipe he was sitting next to while on his lunch break. I wish I could tell you more, but what he had was a clue, but no bombshell."

Roger rubbed his chin. "No. That ain't much, but it's something. That does leave us with who they were and how they got the information."

"It does. I wish he had more, but it's something, and I've faith in you to ferret it out."

"Thanks for the vote of confidence. I could use a few today."

71

"You're welcome, Roger."

Bill's eyes rose to a man who had just walked in the door. Roger could see a look of recognition in his eyes and Bill motioned for the man to come over to their table. Roger turned towards the approaching man, but he didn't know him. Bill seemed to know half the people in the county at any one time. Bill spoke to the man. "Hey, Rick. Good to see you. It's been a while. Have a seat and chew some fat."

Rick said, "Okay, only got time for coffee and a cinnamon roll."

"That'll be fine. Rick, I want you to meet my friend Roger Pyles. I've known this character since we were kids back in the hills of West Virginia and can vouch for his character or lack of it."

Rick said, "I'll fit right in with you two."

Roger said, "Don't believe half of what Bill says about me or for that matter, half of what he says at all. The true part would be how the two of us got ourselves in some real jams together, but the hard part will be determining how much the story has grown and been embellished over the years."

"Yes," Rick said, "With an introduction like that, I'm sure I'll fit right in."

The men laughed at the little joke. Sugar Plum interrupted, filled the empty coffee cups, and got Rick's order. When she left, Rick asked Roger, "Are you the fellow that was involved in the recovery and investigation of the murdered girl up in the Windover Pond?"

Roger nodded. "That would be me. I also helped with the cold case of a dead young woman at a local diner. You may have heard of that one too."

"I have," Rick said. "The first case sure sent a lot of shock waves through my workplace.'

"Interesting," Roger said. "Where do you work?"

"Kennedy Space Center," Rick said.

Bill said, "Roger, Rick's an astronaut I've had the privilege to know."

Roger extended his hand across the table and shook Rick's outstretched hand. Roger said, "It's good to know you. I've sometimes been called an astronaut myself."

"Don't believe him, Rick," Bill said. "He's no astronaut, maybe a wannabe space cadet at best."

Rick laughed, "No question about it. I'm among friends and like-minded people."

"You have me curious, Rick," Roger asked. How did the Pond girl's murder affect you?"

Rick said, "The investigation turned up some things NASA would've liked to remain not talked about. One being how German scientists, some Nazis, were instrumental in getting our space program off the ground. Some of them like Von Braun were caught up in what was going on in Germany before WW II, while others were true believers and guilty of war crimes. It's the latter group NASA finds embarrassing and would like to forget. Your investigation shined some light on that group, and when the second in command was relieved of his duties and then machine-gunned to death in South America, well, your name was on many people's lips and not in a good way."

Roger said, "I see. It's not the first time I've had that same effect on people. That Von Braun fellow used to fly gliders in the area I grew up."

Rick said, "Von Braun was an interesting character. He grew up in a religious family. After a flirt with the Nazis, he became a Christian like I am."

Bill said, "Yeah, I think he had 'The heavens declare the glory of God' on his tombstone."

Rick said, "Psalms 19:1. He wanted to leave a testimony after he was gone. Are you guys believers?"

Roger said, "My late wife was. Bill and me both had some religious training when we were boys."

Bill nodded. "We pretty much treat people as they treat us. I've met a few Christians that rubbed me the wrong way, but they were the exception rather than the rule. It's usually the others you got to watch. As a cop, I rarely run across a religious person I have a problem with and have to deal with."

Rick said, "That's good. I've ran across a number who are hostile, even at NASA."

Roger grunted, "Tell me about it. I was a college professor who was run out of town on a rail because I wanted my students to think and question what they were told. Was it actual fact, a theory, or a belief? Boy oh boy, did I stir up a hornet's nest when we took a serious look at Darwinism Evolution. You would have thought I wanted to shoot the Pope. To quote that famous Southern philosopher and sage, Lewis Grizzard, 'I know a lot of people who are educated far beyond their intelligence.' Is that subject ever a sacred cow you better not question."

Rick said, "Yes, I know what you're saying. That kind of dogmatic thinking is even in NASA. I believe in divine creation. Von Braun did too, but NASA has changed, and he's gone. There're a lot of scientists who see the flaws in Darwin's ideas but are afraid to say so. Some people serve as gatekeepers who'll see their scientific papers are published, they don't get money for research, and get quietly and sometimes not so quietly pushed to the side and even removed for not being in lockstep. You know Roger; I guess I'm a lot like you, open-minded and curious. I was an atheist until I was challenged to do a forensic study on creation and the like. It was after I'd done that, I came to a conclusion we had help getting here, and that first step led me to where I am today. "

Roger said, "I know what you're saying. For me, it was like being a real free thinker in a Nazi or Stalin-like regime. When I used Michael Denton or Richard Milton's works, the college gurus blew a head gasket and did a hit job on me academically and personally. I even used Steven Jay Gould's work to show the flaws, but in the end, I was censored. You sure don't want to point out the flaws in radioactive dating of how old the earth is. I always thought and still do that the greatest strength of science was an openness to debate, but the college in Maryland had other ideas."

Rick said, "So what are you doing now? What brought you down here from the frozen northland?"

Roger got a sour look on his face. "About the time I was in the midst of the problems at the college, my wife and son died in a car wreck. I was devastated, and when the college agreed to settle, I took it. In all honesty, I came here to try to drown my troubles with alcohol. I was doing a good job at it too, till my buddy Bill intervened and got me working with the police on solving cases. I was quite good at that up north."

Rick said, "Sorry to hear of all you've been through. I hope you can make a fresh start in Florida. The world needs people like you. People with a message to tell often have to start with a mess."

Roger looked at Bill. "Well, it hasn't all been smooth sailing. There've been ups and a few downs, but I'm trying to make it."

"That's good," Rick said. "I can't tell you how many of us are thankful for a second, even third and fourth or more, chances."

Sugar Plum appeared with Rick's pastry and coffee. "Here you go. Sorry it took so long. Someone dropped the coffee pot and broke it. What a mess that was, coffee and glass everywhere. And then I had to brew another pot. I'm so sorry."

"That's okay," Rick said. "I got the opportunity to meet some fine gentlemen."

Roger laughed. "I guess you're talking about Bill and me, but it reminds me of an old Three Stooges routine. A man greets them 'Gentlemen, gentlemen,' and they look around behind them to see who came in. They knew it couldn't be them the man was talking to."

Bill said, "Rick, when you get to know us better, you'll see he's right."

Rick said, "Yup, I'm among friends," and laughed.

"I'm gonna leave this love-fest before a fistfight, or a hockey game breaks out. Call me if you need anything. Bye," and Sugar Plum was off.

Bill said, "I think this would be a good time to leave. We've work to do, and you have a delicious pastry to devour. We'll be going."

Bill and Roger got up.

Rick said, "It was sure nice to meet you. I hope to see you again soon."

"Thanks," they said in unison.

Bill said, "Yup, till next time."

They exited the building. Roger said to Bill, "I can't believe we were in there over an hour. Seems like we just sat down."

"Time flies when you're having fun. Roger, I didn't know you were a fan of Lewis Grizzard."

"I am. That country boy makes more sense than a dozen PhDs."

A loud noise to their left got their attention. A Brevard County Sheriff's Department car with the space shuttle stenciled on the side roared by with blue lights flashing, and its siren screaming.

Roger asked Bill, "I wonder what happened. Did you hear anything on the radio?"

"No." He checked it. "No wonder. I didn't have it turned on. Oops." Bill listened for a moment. "The siren stopped. Whatever the event is, it's just around the bend in the road."

"That's about where the bar is, isn't it?"

Bill said, "It is, but it's probably a traffic incident of some sort."

Roger said, "Let's hope it's only that. I'm feeling better, but my head still hurts. Don't think I'm up for heavy-duty cop work today."

Bill replied, "Welcome to my world. You do what you have to. We all do that."

"Guess you're right."

"Let's get going and see what it is."

"Probably won't concern us."

"Let's hope not."

Jay Heavner

## Chapter 16

Traffic slowed as Bill went south on US 1. Several police cars sat in front of the Williams Point Bar and Grill, and there was crime tape blocking the area between the vehicles. Roger's truck was at the center of that area.

Roger looked at Bill with wide eyes. "This don't look good."

Bill said, "No, it don't. You let me do the talking."

"Sure thing."

They drove past the bar and made a U-turn across the median strip. As soon as they pulled in the bar parking lot at a discrete distance, a Brevard County Deputy approached and said, "You guys need to leave. We have an active police investigation going on. Get outta here."

Bill said, "I'm Chief of Police Bill Kenney of the Canaveral Flats Police Department. I can show ID if you like. Looks like you all just got here."

The Deputy grunted, "Bill Kenney, I've heard of you. Who's your sidekick, Tonto?"

Bill Kenney gave the cop a stern look. "My sidekick is also a member of the Canaveral Flats Police Department and if memory serves me right, and I'm sure it does, this little stretch of the highway and area is officially in Canaveral Flats. Now tell me young man, what exactly is happening to warrant all this commotion."

"No need to get huffy," the Deputy said. "It's just not every day you find two bodies in the bed of a pickup truck."

"Really?" said Bill. "What have you established so far?"

78

"Couple of John Does. No visible signs of trauma I could easily see. Lying there like they went to sleep, all peaceful like with their ball hats covering their faces, except they're dead as doornails."

"Think I better have a look," Bill said. "You wait here."

Roger nodded.

Bill got out of his truck and walked over to the other vehicle with the Deputy beside him. Bill looked in the bed of the Roger's truck and then around the area. Roger could tell they were talking, but couldn't make out what they said because of the traffic noise from the busy highway. Bill said something more to the Deputy, and then Bill walked back to his truck and got in. "What's goin' on?" said Roger.

"It would be best if we left quickly and talked in a minute."

"Oh," Roger said.

When they were a mile south, Roger asked, "I don't like the looks of this. What's going on?"

"Something's not right. What I do know for sure is there're two very dead muscular looking men in the back of your truck, and they do look like they went to sleep except they appear to have been strangled. Not sure of it. That's a call for the coroner to make, but that would be my bet. We need to get you home and pretend we didn't stop. I don't think that cop will remember us. I told him the city line was about ten feet south of the crime scene, and it was not under my jurisdiction. My mistake and it was a county matter."

"You know they're gonna run the tags and come looking for me at my house."

"I do, but you have an alibi. You were at the bar till closing, Big Red and yours truly got you from the bar to my place, and then you slept it off on my living room couch till morning and have been with me ever since. That should do it."

Roger said, "I hope so. If things can go wrong, they will. I thought breakfast would cure my hangover, but I believe the shock of the dead men in my truck took care of it. Any idea who they were?"

"Never seen 'em before. Looked like a couple of working stiffs you'd find anywhere."

They turned onto Canaveral Flats Boulevard, passed Miller's Store, and stopped in front of Roger's trailer. Two Sheriff's cars sat in the rutted driveway, little more than two paths worn in the grass. "This doesn't look good," Roger said.

"No it doesn't, Tonto. Just tell them we've been together since late last night which we have."

"Okay," Roger said. "Knock off the Tonto stuff, okay Lone Ranger?"

One deputy took notice of them as they got out of Bill's truck. Roger said, "Hello, there. Can I help you?"

The Deputy asked, "You the owner of this place, a Mister Roger Pyles?"

"I am."

The Deputy said, "I guess you know why I'm here."

Roger said, "Did I need to pull some permits for the electric work?"

"I could care less about whether you pulled permits or not. Besides, this is Canaveral Flats, and you follow city regulations which as far as I know are slim to none or non-existent," the Deputy said. He looked at Bill. "Who are you?"

"I was wondering the same thing. I thought I knew most of the law enforcement in the north end of the county. To answer your question, I'm Canaveral Flat's Chief of Police Bill Kenney. What's going on?"

"911 got a call about a suspicious vehicle in front of a local bar. The officer who responded to the call found two men dead in the vehicle, and that truck's registered to you, Mr. Pyles," the Deputy said, "You got anything to say about this matter?"

Bill spoke up, "He's been with me since late last night. We had a long breakfast at Jimmies and were just getting back."

The Deputy asked, "Jimmies on US 1? So, on your way back, did you see some police activity at the Williams Point Bar?"

Roger said, "We did. We weren't sure what all was going on. I saw my truck behind the police tape and thought it best to let them do whatever it was they were doing and come back later for the truck. Hmm, doesn't sound like I'll get my truck back today. I've worked forensic, and processing takes time. What about my place? Am I okay to be here, or do you need to do something at this location too?"

"You need to stay where you are and not come closer. I'd like the crime lab boys to take a look before you come in. It could be a while."

Roger said, "Have you seen my dog? She's got to be around here someplace. Is she okay?"

The Deputy said, "We found her. She didn't give us any trouble and seemed to have found a bag of dried food to tear into. She's sleeping on the porch now."

Roger said, "That's good to know. Did you see a cat? I have a cat too."

"No cat's been around."

"I'm not surprised. She's a little flighty. Only person she's warmed up to is me. She'll do all right. If she gets hungry, she'll kill something. A lizard or some rodent the world will be better off without anyway. She won't starve."

The Deputy asked again, "So Mister Pyles, where have you been in the last twelve hours?"

"Getting drunk at the Williams Point Bar and Grill."

"For twelve hours?"

Roger said, "I got there in the early afternoon and closed the place down. Fortunately for me, the bouncer, a fella called Big Red, took pity on me and called my buddy Bill here to come and get me. He did, and I slept the night away till this morning on his couch. Then we went to breakfast at Jimmies on US 1. I was gonna pick up my truck after we ate, but the police activity at the bar told us to keep going. The cops weren't there when we drove up. Only on the way back and now I find you guys here. All this has sure thrown a monkey wrench in my plans for today."

The Deputy looked at Bill. "Can you verify this?"

"I can. Big Red told me about his time at the bar, and we loaded him up in my truck a little after two A.M. and brought him to my place. He was so drunk he could barely walk. This morning when Mr. Cheapskate offered to buy breakfast at Jimmies, I jumped on it. It could be a month of Sundays before his generosity might kick in again. He's been with me since about two last night till now."

The Deputy said, "I see. No chance he could have left during the night and returned before you awoke?"

Bill said, "As I said, Roger could barely stand up. I know a falling-down drunk when I see one. If he had wandered out, I would have found him face down in my yard. And besides, he'd have set off my alarm on the way out. I can vouch for his whereabouts."

The Deputy said, "Mr. Pyles. It would be best if you stayed away while we process the area around your house. We'll let you know when you can come back."

Roger said, "Yeah, I understand."

"Where will you be?" the Deputy asked.

"He'll be with me," Bill said, "if anyone needs to locate him."

"Good idea," said the Deputy. "Now you guys best be going so we can do what we need to here. Oh, one more thing, Mr. Pyles. Take off your clothes."

"What?"

"We'll need them for processing."

Roger grunted, "Yeah, guess you're right. For a moment, I thought you were going kinky on me."

The Deputy gave him a dirty look. "You can keep your underwear on."

"Thanks for the small favor." Roger took his shirt, shoes, and pants off and dropped them on the ground.

Bill said, "Okay. Roger, let's go."

Roger nodded and followed Bill back to his truck. He said nothing until they were near Bill's house. "Looks like we have ourselves another confused fiasco, if I may say so."

Bill said, "You may. Something's smelling under this circus tent, and it ain't the elephants."

"And I know it's not Elly the elephant from the Windover case this time."

"Nope, more like the twins, Murder and Mayhem."

"So what's going on, Bill? I'd be a fool to believe in coincidences."

"No, something's up big time. I'm not sure how this puzzle will all fit together, but the pieces are all from the same box, I think."

"You think it all has to do with the body at the river?"

Bill said, "I do, but I can't connect the dots."

"Me neither."

"Roger, for the meantime, I believe it would be best if you stuck close to me."

"Yeah, no argument from me."

Bill said, "You ride around with me while I patrol the town. I'll get you familiar with the ins and outs of our little burg and provide you with an alibi for today if you need one."

Roger said, "Now that I may. And it's a good possibility the cops will need to talk with me."

"Yup. I think you're right."

"Got some clothes for me?"

Bill said. "I think I've got some that will fit. They may be tight. You're a little bigger than I am."

"Thanks for not saying fat, old buddy."

"Roger, if you make any cracks about getting in my pants, I will not accept responsibility for what happens to a certain house guest of mine."

Roger rolled his eyes, "I wouldn't think about it, old buddy." Roger steamed. There was nothing like getting kicked when he was down. What else could go wrong?

# Chapter 17

The Next Day

The old man with the long scar on his face sat on the porch of the second story house by the Indian River. The house was an anomaly, and he liked it that way. It sat on a spit of land on the east side of Indian River Road that jutted out into the river. There were no neighbors on this side, and those on the other side were at the end of long driveways far from the twisting and narrow old river road.

He had a grand view of the mile-wide lagoon. A half-mile to the south, Florida Route 528 crossed the Bennett Causeway and connected the mainland with Merritt Island. He had chosen wisely, when he purchased this land with money smuggled into America from Germany after the war. Who would have ever thought this house would be a safe house for Nazis escaping the Allies, but it was. A boathouse on the east side provided water access to small boats carrying contraband from various places in the world.

The river was so peaceful this morning. It was like glass, and a thin mist moved across the water in places. This would soon disappear with the morning temperature rise. Lives were like those vapors, he thought. Both were only there for a moment in time and soon passed away only remembered by the few who had seen them before they too passed away and were forgotten. The Third Reich was to last a thousand years, and it seemed now like that vapor. We are like the witnesses trying to remember, trying desperately to give life and form back to it.

He and others had worked for decades to resurrect the Reich. They had little to show for it, but the dream remained. The Master Race must rule for the good of all and provide peace for the world and genetic purity for the human race. That was the plan, but so much time had passed, and so much effort had gone into the attempt to raise the dead. Perhaps he should move on, but how could he? It was all he had and all that mattered. He'd dedicated his life to the cause, and he would die for it. Loyalty, honor, and duty.

This Roger Pyles was undoubtedly getting to be a thorn in his flesh. What were the chances of him getting involved with the investigation of the murder of the woman in the pond? Maybe ODESSA should have taken Valentine out when they could have, and all this could have been avoided. Valentine always had been a little bit of a rogue and pushed the limits. He had it good at NASA, but had become cocky and overconfident in his abilities. And now he was dead. His excesses in killing young Jewish girls had been his undoing. He'd been advised to cool it, but he'd ignored the warnings. Why was this Pyles fellow so hard to kill? Blind luck? Good fortune? A guardian angel working overtime? Their best assassin, the Stork, had tried and failed. Maybe it was merely age that was slowing all the old warriors down, including the Stork. And now he was dead, and Stiltsville was gone. That den of iniquity had been a great moneymaker for the cause. Money could be laundered easily at the bar and bordello. Politicians could be bribed and blackmailed because of the activities it offered. And now, it was gone, and Roger Pyles still lived.

Why? He had a way of getting in the way and finding ways to cause trouble for them. The old man's stomach felt sore. He took another drink of his German-made beer, Becks, and looked at the waters. The wind was picking up, and waves were starting to stir the water up. The heist at the Treasure Museum had gone well, and now the loot was on a private yacht that would soon leave for South America.

Roger Pyles. That name kept coming up. It was a pity that no one on the burglary team was a trained killer. He had to send two hired local knucklehead brutes out to get him. Perhaps it was better they were dead. They sure messed up trying to get the information out of the third member. He knew that man, the smartest one of the three, knew where the Queen's jewels were, and the other two had not gotten the information, but had killed him and lost the body. And it had turned up and was drawing unwanted and unnecessary attention. And

Roger Pyles was involved with that. Who had killed the two men? He had thought about the situation. They were liabilities that needed silencing in the near future. Someone had silenced them, but who?

Certainly not Roger Pyles. Why had the killer or killers placed the dead men in the back of Roger Pyles truck? His stomach churned some more, and he took a big gulp of Becks to try to silence it. It didn't work. Roger Pyles seemed to have more lives than a cat. Or luck. He wondered if Roger Pyles gambled. He would not want to bet against him, but the cards showing told him eventually Roger Pyles would have to be dealt with – win, lose, or draw were the only options, and he couldn't afford to lose many more hands to Roger Pyles, and his guardian angel. Loyalty, honor, and duty unto death for the cause no matter whose death it was.

# Chapter 18

"Mr. Smith, that sure was fun," she said.

"Which do you mean, my wife? The sex or the little adventure close to home?"

"Both. The adventure got my blood racing. It felt like old-times, only this was practically in our back yard, not half way around the world as usual."

"Yes, that does seem strange. Do what needs to be done and then be home in under ten minutes."

She said, "And the delegation was pleased with the way we handled the situation?"

"I spoke to D personally. He and the others were pleased."

"I haven't had to kill a bad guy in a long time."

"Me neither. Those two never knew what hit them."

Mr. Smith said, "Especially the one you took out. You stalked him like a tiger. It's no wonder they call you the 'Cat.'"

She smiled, "I do like that name. With big lugs like that, they're usually strong as an ox, but with the same brainpower. This guy was no exception. I'm glad he wasn't like the one we encountered in Crimea. It took both of us to neutralize him."

He nodded, "How well I remember him. He was a worthy foe. Too bad he chose to be a mercenary working for the Russians."

"Yes, too bad. He paid for his wrong choice."

"Don't we all?" he said. "I'm glad it went without a hitch."

"What about the Indian who showed up unannounced last

night? He sure was stealthy. He could have taught me a few things, I think."

"I have to admit that it was creepy and strange. That brown man with long straight hair with a leather headband. I think it was alligator. And almost naked wearing only a loincloth and moccasins. How did he ever appear like a phantom right after we killed those two thugs?"

She said, "Yes, it was incredible, and did you notice how disarming he was? He simply raised his hand and said 'Peace to you.'"

He shook his head. "I've never seen anything like it. He shows up out of nowhere, say 'Peace,' and we don't automatically try to kill him. That's strange beyond odd. And he didn't seem concerned at all about seeing two dead bodies."

She said, "It definitely wasn't his first rodeo. And the next thing he said was even stranger, 'They needed killing.' How did he know?"

"I don't know, but his voice said he was sure of himself on that. And then it got even stranger. The dog walked right up to him, no growling, nothing, and sat at his feet. The Indian looked down, called her by name, K9, and then began to stroke her head. She was as much at peace with him as we were. She looked at the bodies and whimpered. He said to her, 'It okay, K9. It necessary. Cry no more,' and she didn't. She walked to the porch, went in through the doggie door, laid down, and went to sleep. And then he smiled that awkward smile and said, 'And now, I leave you. You have work.'"

"Yes," she said. "He vanished like a phantom. I never saw anything like it. Glad he was friendly."

"I'm not sure if he was friendly or didn't have a dog in the fight. He'd be a good one to have on your side. I remember the days before I had all my training on fighting. When I'd go to a bar, I'd always make friends with the bouncer or bouncers. It got me out of a few jams in the old days. Plus, I learned a lot by watching them interact with people, the sober and the not, the happy drunks and the belligerent ones. Bouncers learn very fast how to size them up, and I learned how big fellows like him would fight by watching the fights. It helped in our little encounter the other night."

"Yes, they could have been dangerous as big as they were, but all they had was their bulk and brute strength, nothing more."

Mr. Smith said, "Agreed. I'm glad it went as well as it did. Strangling them with that soft garrote would leave no visible marks on the necks and the twists done to the neck make for quick killing."

She said, "Any coroner worth his salt will figure out what happened during the autopsy."

"You're correct. The how is easy, but the whodunit and why is a whole different ballgame. And we went to great lengths to see they never find out."

"What about ODESSA? They'll try to answer those questions."

He said, "They will, but we covered our tracks well. They'll still be guessing. My guess is they'll write these two off as collateral damage and find some more expendable muscle-bound dummies to do their dirty work. Never bring in the heavy artillery unless you have to. Just like in the war, their resources aren't infinite."

"Like in the heist?"

"Yes, like in the museum heist."

"But they got away with the treasure they took."

He smiled, "They did, but you know what they say; the show ain't over till the fat lady sings."

"I thought you might know more than you were saying on that. And I liked your idea of placing the bodies in Roger's truck."

"After dealing with those two who had been sent to eliminate old Roger, we might as well make use of the remains. The gators at

90

our place were full from other business we had, so I thought, why not give ODESSA something to think about and why not put all the eyes on Roger. I wanted him too hot to handle. No one would mess with him while he was in the limelight, and I wanted him to be on his toes. There're some seriously big sharks in the waters he's swimming in, and we can't protect him all the time. He needs to be wary and ready for whatever may come his way."

"He does."

They were quiet for a moment, and she snuggled up next to his body. "Husband," she purred. "All this pillow talk has me aroused. Are you aroused too?"

He put his arm around her, "No, but you know how a man's made. I can be there in no time flat. Just do what you always do to light my fire."

She hugged him tight and began to caress his bare chest. "This a good start?"

"It is." He turned on his side and kissed her lips. "Ready when you are."

She smiled, "Well, ring my chimes."

"You know how corny that sounds?"

"I do. Now, are you going to ring them or not?"

He did. Twice.

## Chapter 19

"You know, I'm getting tired of seeing your ugly face."

"You should talk. You're no beauty queen yourself."

"I want a divorce."

"Don't let the door hit you on the way out."

"Just wish I could go home."

Bill said, "You got your wish. The county Mounties called and said they were done processing your truck. If I were you, I'd stop at a car wash, and pressure wash the outside and pay extra to have the interior thoroughly cleaned out. Your truck needed it beforehand, and after the cops have been all over it and the two dead bodies in the bed, you better have it scrubbed real good."

Roger said, "I can tell why you never got married. Who could put up living with you? I've only had to stay with you three days as a guest, and I feel like I've been living an Odd Couple black comedy routine. And you got some horrible taste in clothing."

"You should talk. I can't see what your wife saw in you."

"She loved me for better or worse."

Bill said, "Thank God I don't have to. If your house hadn't been a possible crime scene, and your truck one for sure, and you needing watched over for your protection, and good old me feeling sorry for you, I'd have let you stir in your own juices, ole buddy."

Roger said through clenched teeth, "Thanks."

The two men said nothing more for a moment or two.

Roger looked at his shoes. "So, you gonna take me down to the police vehicle impound so I can get my truck and be out of your hair?"

"In a heartbeat. Let's go."

"Right now? No fifteen minute warning like my wife would've given me?"

"Nope. Let's go."

"Bill, my day's looking up."

Bill grunted, "Mine too."

They walked to Bill's truck, got in and drove through the rutted and washboard streets of Canaveral Flats to Roger's trailer. They parked at the gate. The chain was dummy-locked as usual. Roger opened it, and they walked down the short lane to the trailer. Crime scene tape blocked their way.

Roger looked at Bill. "Guess it's okay to remove this?"

"Yeah," Bill said. "The investigators gave the okay. You're free to roam around your trailer and property."

"Just like my critters."

"Yup, just like your critters, but don't get in any more trouble."

Roger said, "I wouldn't think of it. You know me."

Bill rolled his eyes. "Yeah, I do."

 K9 came out to greet them. She wagged her tail and went to Roger, who patted her head. "Good dog," he said. She looked at Bill and growled. Roger looked at Bill, and a sly smile came to Roger's face. He said, "Good dog," as he rubbed her head.

Bill ignored the slight. "The place don't look too bad. No worse than it was before. It does look like a struggle could have taken place. Look how the weeds and grass are matted. I see a bush with a broken branch, but I don't see any blood, though."

"Yeah, I see it too, but like you said, no blood. You think those two goons were here to beat me up or worse?"

Bill scratched his head. "If I were a betting man, I'd say yeah. And I'd bet it was the worse option they had planned for you. Roger, your guardian angels are working overtime. Hope you appreciate them whoever they are. Those two lugs looked threatening even when I saw them lying dead in the back of your truck."

"You know who they are yet?"

"Yeah, the investigators got hold of the bar owner who got hold of Big Red. He ID'ed them as two laborers he had seen working out at the launch pad. Their fingerprints confirmed he was correct. They were a couple of minor league thugs with long rap sheets consisting of a lot of petty crimes, drugs, drunk driving, dealing in stolen goods, that kind of stuff. Looks like they were trying to up their game and came up losers big time."

Roger said, "I'm glad they did. I still got lots of people to annoy before they throw dirt in my face."

Bill grunted.

Roger said, "What's so funny?"

"You? Annoying? I never noticed."

Roger gave Bill some directions on where he could go, which only made Bill laugh. Roger growled, but said no more.

They walked around the place looking for anything out of place. Roger said, "I don't see any damages to the trailer. If anything, it looks better. Lester must have got the electrical work done and swept out the place too."

"Good old Lester," said Bill.

Roger flipped a couple of switches and lights came on. "Yeah, Lester's been busy. Wonder what this handy work will cost me?"

Bill said, "A whole lot less than a licensed electrician would have cost, and I can guarantee the work will be as good, and I'm not saying that because he signs my paycheck."

"Sounds like I got a deal. Think I should go over to his house and pay him?"

"Roger, I don't think you need to hurry over. He don't need the money, and he'll come around when he wants it. Besides, he's got a girlfriend, and he spends as much time at her house as his own."

"Why that old fox. He may have snow on the roof, but sounds like he's still got fire in the furnace."

Bill laughed, "No, that old bird ain't dead yet. Hey, look the inside over and lock the door when you come out. I know you usually don't, but I think you better start doing so. That flimsy door will at least keep the honest out, and the dishonest will at least leave some marks when they break-in."

"Good idea, Bill. Just give me a minute or two to check on the inside and then will be outta here."

"Okay." Bill sat down in a chair on the screened-in porch. K9 growled at him, but without much enthusiasm. Bill grinned. "Yeah, I like you too, K9. Keep an eye on Roger. He needs it." The dog lay down, closed her eyes, sighed, and quickly fell asleep."

Roger came out and said, "Hey, you want a beer?"

"I do, but I'm on duty, and we've got things to do. You want a beer?"

"Well, it's been three days since I've had one. Let's see if I can make it four. You know, one day at a time."

Bill nodded, "Yuppers, one day at a time."

# Chapter 20

The boys got in Bill's truck and headed for the police impound yard.

Roger said to Bill, "After three days with me tied to your hip, it almost feels like I'm married to you."

Bill said, "Now that's a disgusting thought. It was bad enough just as Felix and Oscar."

"The Odd Couple." Roger laughed. "That's a funny show. It's a lot more fun watching than living for three days."

"Very true," Bill said. He paused to change mental gears. "Roger, I have a personal question for you. Mind if I ask?"

"If it's, 'do I want to ever cohabitate with you ever again,' the answer is an emphatic no."

Bill chuckled, "That wasn't the question, but I agree with the answer 100%. The heavy-duty question I have is, what makes you happy?"

"Drinkin'."

"Drinkin'?"

"Yeah."

"Yeah? Could you please tell me more?"

Roger was silent for a moment. "Well, it's not drinking that makes me happy. I was happy when I had my wife and son, even when I was going through the problems at the college. I drink to ease the pain of my loss, so I guess drinking makes me happy."

"You know I deal with a lot of people with problems."

Roger said, "Is this gonna be one of your feel-good stories?"

"Probably. Do you want to hear it?"

"I don't think I have a choice, but if it makes you feel better, go ahead."

Bill felt like saying something, but bit his tongue. After his initial hesitation, he started. "As you well know, the warm climate here makes sleeping outdoors tolerable year-round, and we get a lot of homeless people coming to Florida because of it. One day this guy appeared along US 1, and he was trying to sell his hand-drawn art to make some money. This state has a long history of people selling roadside art. The paintings made by the group that came to be known as the Highwaymen are quite prized today. His art wasn't nearly as good. I stopped and when he realized I was a cop, he got a little nervous. We talked a little. I just wanted to know who he was. You know, I was merely keeping my finger on the pulse of what was going on in Canaveral Flats. He told me he'd been harassed by cops in his travels sometimes when he tried to sell his stuff.

"When he saw I wasn't goin' give him a hard time, he relaxed. They usually do at that point. I asked him how it was going, and he said not so good. He hadn't sold anything all day. I asked him if he was hungry, and he said yes. I was on my way home and had picked up a pizza. I asked him if he wanted some. He asked if it had anchovies. I told him no. It was pepperoni, and he said, it didn't matter. He hated anchovies, but he was hungry enough to eat whatever it was. I gave him three slices, and he took a bite. He called to someone in the bushes. Another man came out, and he shared his newfound bounty with him. I gave them three more slices of pizza that they ate. They were most thankful.

"They were traveling together, safety in numbers, you know. Steve, the artist, told me they were both Vietnam veterans down on their luck. Now Steve could have eaten all three slices and never told his companion, but he didn't. The man had a generous heart. I gave them some information on how to get some help. Our county has a good group of ex-military that try to help people in those guys'

97

situations. I heard through the grapevine, the veteran's group was able to find them a place to stay, and they were doing all right today. I was glad I could be a little help to those guys."

"You helped them pull themselves up by their bootstraps," Roger said.

"You have to have boots before you can do that."

"Very true." A car went around them at a high rate of speed. Roger said, "Ain't you going after him?"

"Nah. County boys will get him. They're running a speed trap just around the bend in the road about a mile or so south. Just wait. He's about to be blessed with a ticket."

"Bet you've met some interesting characters in the years you've been a cop."

Bill said, "Some I remember and some I'd like to forget. I've met a few smart ones, but a lot of dumb ones too, and I've heard a lot of crazy stories I swear are true. I couldn't make this stuff up."

"Ever thought of writing a book?"

"Now and then, but you'd have to be nuts to want to do that. Seems like there's always someone complaining about something an author wrote they didn't like. They could never write a book, but they sure could grumble about someone who could."

Roger asked, "If you did write a book, what would you call it?"

"Well, let's see. Hmm. How about Crime for Dummies or maybe America's Dumbest Criminals? Those two would make great titles."

"They would. In your opinion, what makes a dumb criminal?"

Bill replied, "That's pretty easy. A dumb criminal is one who acts dumb. They're greedy, selfish, ignorant, and just plain mean and don't use the good sense God gave them. Don't get me started."

As they rounded a bend in the road, they could see blue lights flashing. A deputy had a motorist, the one who had passed them at a high rate of speed, pulled over and was writing a ticket. Bill said, "Rule Number One, obey the laws, and you won't run into trouble with the law, and Rule Number Two, never give the cop a hard time. I've given a lot of people breaks who were respectful."

"I bet most of them were women."

Bill said, "They were. Women are usually smarter than men on these matters."

"Plus they cry."

"Yeah, I've had my crying women."

Roger said, "You think it would work for me?"

"You ever try it?"

"No, but my wife did with me in the passenger's seat. The cop let her off."

"Roger, don't try it. They'll think you're a weirdo and haul you in for sure."

"I thought so. That's why I never tried it."

"You're no dummy like that hot-rodder in the car. See how he's yelling at the cop. He's getting a ticket and if he keeps it up, maybe a ticket to the gray bar motel till he cools down. Always be courteous to the cops. It's the biggest factor in whether you get a ticket for a simple traffic infraction. He's dumb and probably too dumb even to realize how dumb he is. I don't think those guys who robbed the museum were dumb crooks. I think they were pros."

"I do too. So tell me some funny stories about dumb criminals. Got any traffic stop tales?"

Bill said, "A whole bunch. Truth is stranger than fiction. Try this one. Late one night, I saw a classic car whipping along at a high rate of speed. It was a '64 Buick in mint condition traveling at fifty miles over the limit. I got after him, and it seemed he wanted to make a run for it, but thought better and changed his mind. I approached the car carefully. An old guy of at least eighty, probably more, sat in the driver's seat and he appeared quite agitated.

"I asked him if he knew how fast he was going and he told me of course he did, and it was an emergency, so I asked him what kind of a medical emergency it was. His face reddened, and he repeated it was an emergency. I asked him again what the emergency was, and he said, 'I can't tell you. You'll laugh.' So, I told him if he'd tell me what the emergency was, I wouldn't write him a ticket. He made me promise not to laugh."

Roger said, "This is getting interesting. So, what happened?"

Bill said, "He said, "Well son, man to man, I'm eighty-four years old and I ain't had an erec-uh...well, I haven't been in the mood for love in years and I'm in the mood right now, and on my way to my girlfriend's house! I was stunned for a moment. I'd never heard that excuse before, and well, man to man, I had to empathize with the old guy, so I gave him a police escort to his destination."

Roger said, "I can't believe this."

"It's all true. I swear it. He hopped out of his car with a spring in his step, ran straight to me, and shook my hand and thanked me three times. Then he ran to the open door and into the arms of a smiling elderly woman. The door shut and I could see them kissing up a storm. He noticed me watching and gave a thumbs up which I returned. Then he pulled the blind down. You can imagine the rest."

"Yeah, two happy campers."

"Yup."

Roger said, "You should have saved that one for the finale."

Bill said, "Ain't even close. You got me started, and we've some miles to go. Prepare to be entertained."

Roger laughed, "I'm all ears. Tickle my funny bone."

"Okay, Roger. You asked for it. If you die laughing, it's not my fault. You were warned."

"Go for it. Slay me with your cop stories."

"Did you hear the one about the snappin' turtle?"

# Chapter 21

"Well, we had a sweet young thing that lived here in Canaveral Flats. This fellow from Titusville thought he was in love with her, but the feeling wasn't mutual. After a few dates, she tried to let him down gently, but he didn't take it too well. Fact is, he was fuming. He stormed out of her house and wandered around our little town looking for something to strike back at her. He found his weapon, seized it, and went after her with it."

Roger said, "Are you trying to tell me he attacked her with a snappin' turtle?"

"Bingo. I was riding around patrolling, and I saw him chasing her with the reptile which refused to bite her. I stopped, disarmed or should I say, deturtled him, and made the first ever arrest for assault with a deadly assault turtle. The story does have a happy ending though, sorta. He got off with a fine and a warning to stay away from her which he did, and the girl was so grateful to the snapper for not bitin' her, she made a pet out of the turtle, and the last I heard, they, the cute girl and the cute turtle, were living happy together hereafter somewhere in the little town of Christmas where she moved shortly after the reptilian incident."

"Attack with an assault turtle. That had to be a first. This state sure has some strange characters and strange incidents in all kinds of places with strange names, Christmas for one. How did it get its name?"

Bill said, "It goes back to the Seminole Wars. The US Army soldiers built the fort on Christmas Day. Orange County has built a nice reconstructed fort in a county park over there. You ought to go some time."

"Maybe I will. Sounds like a good place to take a date."

"It is." Bill paused. "This state's full of all kinds of names –

Indian names hard to pronounce, space names, and names of other places around the world."

Roger said, "I've run across a few, Econlockhatchee, Apalachicola, Lake Tohopekaliga, for example here. Seems Indian names are everywhere. We had Allegheny, Monongahela, and Appalachian up in our home area."

"Very true. As much as we know about the past, there's a lot more we don't know. Who was here before the people we call Indians? What happened to them?"

Roger said, "That's where archaeology comes in. Someday, we may know more about what was stumbled onto at the Windover site."

"True. And we got space names, Satellite Beach, Venus, and Jupiter. And worldly names like Venice, Naples, and Marathon. Historic names too."

"It's an interesting state," Roger said. "Tell me some more stories. I'm enjoying them."

"Okay. Most criminals try their best not to get arrested, but there are some exceptions. There was a fellow who lived over by US 1 we'd had some problems with. He was a young fellow. Been arrested a few times as a juvenile, a troublemaker and his life could go good or bad at this point. I got a phone call, and the caller asked for me, Chief of Police Bill Kenney. I could barely hear the caller and asked him to speak up. He whispered, 'This is Steve Lindner.' I asked him why he was speaking so quiet and told him there was a warrant for his arrest. He said he knew and wanted to turn himself in right now. He was at his home. In the background, I could hear a strange pounding, a boom, boom, boom, like someone pounding. He said he wanted to surrender, and I needed to come right now.

"I got there in a jiffy and found an angry father and son trying to get in Steve's house. Seems Steve had been messing with the man's daughter, and they wanted to let him know, in no uncertain terms, he was to leave her alone. Turning himself in was his way of getting police protection. Guess he figured jail time was better than five minutes alone with his adversaries."

Roger said, "Yeah, that would seem to be the lesser of the two evils. Did you have any more encounters with him?"

"No. He got out and when he heard the father and son still wanted their pound of flesh from him, he somehow finagled his way on a ship bound for parts unknown. That was the last I heard of him. I don't know if he's still on a ship somewhere or he started a new life somewhere in this big world other than Canaveral Flats. I hope he learned something good from his close calls and took the straight and narrow road henceforward."

Roger laughed, "We learn from our mistakes. Guess that's why I keep making mistakes so I can learn from them."

Bill gave Roger a dirty look. "It's best to learn from other's mistakes."

"True. Give me one more good one, a real gut-buster."

Bill said, "A real gut buster? It's hard to pick. I've seen and heard so many. I've got a million."

"Just a great one now. Save the rest for some time later."

"I can do that. Let's see. Oh, I've got a good one, and it involves someone you know." Bill paused. "You know where the laundromat is in Port St. John?"

"Yeah, up by the plaza."

"That's the one."

"Fellow moved down here from NYC by the name of Jack Grace. Seemed he'd been in trouble there for exposing himself in the Big Apple."

Roger chucked, "A Jumpin' Jack Flasher."

"We had several complaints but nothing we would pin on him. I found him wandering around the plaza and from the looks of him, he'd got worked over by someone he shouldn't have been messin' with. He had a big red bump above his right eye, his lip was split, and his face was all red. His head had a couple of lumps too. I asked him what happened, and he told me through a clenched jaw, he'd been beat up. I asked who done it and he said some woman at the laundromat. A woman did that? He said yes. I thought maybe he'd been in fight with a girlfriend or something like that. We walked over to the laundromat and looked in the windows. Several women were inside.

"I asked which one beat him up. He didn't know. Claimed he never saw her face. That seemed very strange, so I told him to wait outside, and I'd go inside and sort this out. When I went in, one of the women said, 'Officer, thank God you're here. Some crazed man came in about ten or so minutes ago, pulled his T-shirt over his head, and dropped his pants.' The other woman added, 'And he weren't wearin' no underwear, either!' I was beginning to see a picture. I smiled and asked what happened next. One of the women responded, he said, 'Hey girls, ever seen one of these before?' And Connie says, 'Yeah, it does kinda look like a penis, only much smaller.' Then the first woman tells me Connie reached out and grabbed him by the hair of his head that is, and commenced to knocking the livin' hell out of him. That part was obvious.

"My informant continued, 'His arms were over his head in the shirt, and he couldn't do nothin'. It was all over in under a half minute.' She added with a large degree of satisfaction, 'You don't mess with Connie.'"

Roger said, "Is that the Connie at the library?"

"One and the same."

"Bill, you dog. That's the one you tried to set me up with. That old cougar could have killed me. To say the least, that woman's substantial."

"Nah, she'd let you off with a good thrashin'. Besides, I figured you were smart enough to stay away from her claws and clutches. And you were."

"Thanks, old buddy."

Bill said, "You're welcome. Now back to the story. I went outside, cuffed Jack, and arrested him for indecent exposure. He put up a fuss about him being the victim, and why didn't I arrest the woman who did this to him. I reminded him he told me he didn't see her face, but if he wanted to go back in and figure out who done it, I'd wait outside. He shrugged his shoulders, said 'Uhh...never mind.'

"He kept staring through the window at Connie, who was calmly folding her clothes. So I told him that was fine with me. I took him to the back door of the jail, and the boys there took care of the rest."

"Bill, my sides hurt. No more. Could you hold off telling me any more for now? Later would be fine with me."

"Okay, we're almost here. Oh, and by the way, some people want to talk to you."

Roger looked at Bill suspiciously. "And who would that be?"

# Chapter 22

Bill said, "The Coroner for one, and Hernandez for two, and maybe even Marsha for three. Are you up for it? Can you remember and handle all that?"

"Of course," said Roger. "You know me."

"Yeah, I do. That's why I asked if you could do that."

"Not funny, Bill. I may have my problems, but I'm not a total nincompoop." He stopped and grinned, "Well, maybe 10% nincompoop, okay?"

"Yeah Roger, you do have your problems. We all do, but you've got so much on the ball, it's a crying shame when you trip and fall. Are you going to get up this time?"

Roger said nothing for a moment. "Yeah, I am. People need me more than I need myself. Guess you're only really down when you stay down."

That wasn't the answer Bill had hoped for, but it would have to do for now.

"Hey," Roger said. "You tell me I'm a nincompoop. Shouldn't we have turned on 520 and gone over to Merritt Island?"

Bill shook his head. "I see there's still much you don't know. The impound yard's down in Rockledge next to the Coroner's office, not by the Sheriff's office on Merritt Island. That's the vehicle maintenance depot you're thinking of."

"Oh," said Roger. "I saw all the vehicles and assumed that was the impound office, but there was a lot of regular vehicles there. Most didn't have county markings."

"Well, the Sheriff's department does have a bunch of unmarked vehicles, but the county does too. It's a lot of extra expense to paint all of them. Besides, sometimes the county wants stealth. You know how nothing causes drivers to act responsibly like a marked cop car. Sometimes you want people to act natural and not be on their best behavior."

"Bill, you're right. I assumed too much. It's an easy thing to do. It's an easy trap to fall in – judging stuff on how we think they should be rather than questioning what we see." Roger laughed.

"What's so funny, Roger?"

"Oh, the Wright brothers."

"You lost me."

"Back in the early 1900s, the world refused to open their eyes and examine the evidence that was plainly in sight. Two bicycle mechanics in a remote mid-western prairie town confounded the Know-it-all elite east coast publishers and intellectuals. Everyone who knew anything knew a man couldn't fly. Eyewitness reports were scoffed at. The brothers were called hoaxers by no less than the Scientific American magazine and the newspaper standard-bearer, the New York Herald. Even our Army said it was impossible. This phenomenon has occurred with regularity throughout the history of science and technology. I know a healthy skepticism is a good thing, but it's easy to misinterpret the evidence that's right in front of us. Thanks for the reminder, Bill."

He said, "I didn't know that. It's kind of funny to think how the smart people could be so wrong about manned flight especially being so close to Kennedy Space Center and seeing all the rockets launched."

"You know there are still people that deny we went to the Moon. They say it was all done on a movie stage in New Mexico. It's called dissonance. Discomfort is triggered whenever evidence is presented that conflicts with someone's strong-held beliefs, ideas, or values, and people find ways to deal with it. They can deny, try to get the other person to change his viewpoint, ridicule, even reject and derogate him. They got rid of me at the college because I was thinking outside the box and daring to challenge their sacred cows. They found this painful and intolerable, so I had to be dealt with. It's sad, but true. Failing to see what's before our eyes is far from rare. Sad, but true."

"Roger?"

"What?"

"Don't give up. Keep thinking. The world needs people like you and the Wright brothers."

"Galileo got the third degree too. And Roentgen was dismissed by the great Lord Kelvin when he announced his discovery of X-rays."

"Roger, sounds like you're in good company."

"Thanks, Bill for the compliment, but thanks for help in reminding me that things may or may not be as we think they are. It's humbling and always good to remember."

"You're welcome. Roger, we're a block away from the impound office. I'll hang around and make sure you can get your truck. I'd hate to drop you off, leave, and then you find some glitch has happened and you can't get it."

"Thanks, Bill. It could happen."

But this day it didn't. Everything was in order. All the i's were dotted and all the t's crossed. Roger gave Bill a thumb up, and they drove away. Roger went next door to the Coroner's office and watched as Bill's truck disappeared down the street. He wondered what the Coroner had found. Keep an open mind and keep your eyes open to possibilities.

# Chapter 23

Roger rang the entry button to the Coroner's office. He waited a moment for someone to acknowledge he was there. A young woman in protective clothing appeared and looked him over. The outside intercom crackled, "Who is it? State your business, please."

"Is Will here? Tell him Roger Pyles is outside looking in."

"Will's busy. Could you come back later?"

Roger said, "Would you please relay that I'm here? He wants to see me."

"Okay," she said and disappeared. Roger shifted uneasily in the Florida heat. He just hoped it wasn't going to rain. The sky looked threatening, and the normally sweltering heat and humidity seemed even worse than usual. After what seemed an eternity, Will appeared in protective clothing. He looked out at Roger, stripped off his purple rubber gloves, threw them in a bio-hazard bag, and then pressed a button. The secure outer door buzzed. Roger pulled the handle and walked into the outer office open to the public.

"Sure is hot out there today. You could cook an egg on the sidewalk," Roger said.

"Sorry to keep you waiting, Roger. I was busy in the back and in a place where I couldn't stop. I'd shake your hand, but I need to scrub it first. You don't want to know where it was a few minutes ago."

"No problem. Get yourself cleaned up and presentable."

"Will do," Will laughed. "Hey, I made a funny."

"Roger that," Roger said and smiled.

Will smiled too and began to remove his protective clothing. He placed the pieces in the bio-hazard bag, walked to the sink, and

110

scrubbed his hands and arms to the elbows. He turned to Roger, "Looks like you got my message."

"Yeah, Bill passed it on. I was in the neighborhood pickin' up my truck, and so I'm killing two birds with one stone. How's the assistant working out?"

Will said, "Jessica? She's definitely a keeper. She learns real fast. I hope she stays. You know how it is. Get a good one, train them, and they move on to another job that pays better. Did she give you a hard time at the door?"

"Only a little. Seems you were busy and not to be disturbed."

"Roger, I'm getting a lot more done with her running interference for me. That and two can get much more done working together. I'll see she knows who you are and have my blessings always to come in."

"Thanks. I won't have to wait in the heat."

Will sighed, "Oh, the heat. It's been doing a number on the bodies coming in. Decomposition has been bad lately. Had to pick up a body the Palm Bay Police found behind a storage unit. It was a real stinker so bad we weren't sure the sex at first. We were working on him when you came in. A young male with a gunshot wound to the head. Shot execution style. Probably drug related."

"That wouldn't surprise me. What news do you have for me?"

"A bunch. The floater we found in the Indian River, I was able to identify by his fingerprints. He had a record. Nothing too serious. Some DWI's, minor drug offenses, and a breaking and entering. Just enough nastiness to get him on the County Mounties' watch list and in the system. Now here's where it gets interesting. Those two men we found in your truck were known associates of his. We had their prints on records too. Your friend, Big Red identified them first. He got called to the bar while they were still assuming room temperature. I heard him tell the cops about your whereabouts that night. I think you're in the clear. You're a person of interest in this case, but not much. Big Red told the police they were members of the Laborer's Union and all had been working out at a launch pad at the Cape."

"That's interesting," said Roger. "What more can you tell me?"

"They were strangled with some sort of a garrote, and whoever did it knew what they were doing. There were few marks on them which was odd with that kind of a weapon. Usually, the neck is cut severely by the wire, and there's lots of blood, but not in this case. It was a something much softer, but just as efficient, maybe more so. I did find some spots on their necks like little pinpricks. I think they could have been used to inject a fast-acting tranquilizer, but I doubt if toxicity testing would find anything. Looked like the big boys tried to put up a struggle, but it was of no avail to them. The killers were efficient and left few clues. Oh, I did find a fingerprint of one of our dead men matched one found at my father's house where the burglary was."

"And it was probably done in my yard?"

"Cops seem to think so."

Roger said, "And no one saw anything. Amazing."

"Like I said, those two thugs ran into people who knew what they were doing. It's gonna take a streak of luck to find their killers."

"I'd like to find them, and thank them. Most likely, they saved my life."

"I'd been leaning in that direction, Roger. Oh, here's something else interesting. You remember the guy I was telling you about with the pecker implant and no fingerprints?"

"Yeah. What have you got?"

"We got lucky. The manufacturer kept good records. It was installed in a hospital in New York City in a fellow named George Snell who resided in the city. A little checking with the police led to a call from the Feds, yeah, the FBI. George Snell was an alias for a man they suspected of being a career criminal with ties to the Third Reich."

"Why didn't they pick him up?"

Will said, "They knew about him, but were watching him to see if he would lead them to some bigger fish. And now he turns up here, and we just had a huge theft in Cape Canaveral, and it's all coincidence, right?"

"When pigs fly," Roger said. "How did he die?"

"He was suffocated with a pillow at the hotel. I found little pieces of foam in his respiratory tract, some barely detectable bruising, and minor hemorrhaging in the eyes. If not for that, I'd have thought it was natural causes. This also was done by a professional."

"Hmm. I see a pattern here. Dead bodies killed by a pro or pros. Thefts. And Nazis. But how does it all fit together?"

"That, Sherlock, is where you come in. I deal with the dead. They don't talk, but they can sure tell you a whole bunch."

"You-betcha," Will said.

"You-betcha? Are you from Minnesota?"

"Close but no cigar. Not the land of Lake Wobegon, but next door in Wisconsin. Clark County. 60,000 cows, 10,000 people, one stop light and produces 10% of the nation's butter. I'm a hick from the northern sticks."

Roger said, "No wonder we hit it off. I'm a country boy from West Virginia come down here to escape my problems. You?"

"After the heat in Vietnam, I like to froze to death in Wisconsin, so I decided to find someplace warmer. I was vacationing in Orlando doing the theme parks and took a side trip to the rocket ranch, better known as Kennedy Space Center. I saw an ad that the county needed someone with coroner experience. I applied, and the

113

rest is history."

"Interesting story. Guess everyone has one, even the dead."

Will said, "Yeah, the dead do tell tales."

At that time, Jessica came through a door that led to the work area. "All done chief, but I want you to look at something I found."

Will said, "Okay. Jessica, this is Roger Pyles. He's one of us. If he shows up again, let him in. No need to clear it with me."

"Sure boss," she said and returned to the work area.

Will said, "She's got a strong work ethic."

Roger said, "And cute too."

Will grinned. "Yeah, she's cute. You should see her when she's got both arms up to her elbows in a cadaver."

Roger rolled his eyes. "That's quite a mind picture."

"Hey Roger, I need to see what she found. I got to go. Hit the button by the door and let yourself out. Got to go. Bye"

"Okay, till next time. Bye."

Will walked to the door of the work area and disappeared inside. Roger hit the exit door button and left the building. It had been an interesting day so far, and he knew he needed to touch base with Agent Hernandez. He'd better go see her and swap information. He wondered what she knew that he didn't.

# Chapter 24

It was pouring cats and dogs as Roger drove over the high-level bridge from Cocoa to Merritt Island. He took a left onto State Route 3, AKA Courtenay Parkway. The rain started to let up as he passed Merritt Island High School and quit all together shortly before he reached the Publix Super Market. The Sun was shining, and the ground was completely dry. Not a drop had fallen here. "Florida," Roger said to himself. "Gotta love it. Don't like the weather, wait a minute."

Roger saw the RaceTrac gas station on the right side of the highway. He got in the left lane and then the turning lane in the middle. He waited for heavy traffic to pass. A quick look at his watch told him why, 11 o'clock. The drawbridge over the barge canal had been open and just closed. The pent up traffic was surging south. He waited for it to pass, but some traffic coming off the Beeline Expressway merging on Courtenay Parkway kept him waiting. He saw a short break in traffic and accelerated to beat the oncoming vehicles. To his surprise, his tires squealed, and he saw where he'd left some rubber on the road. "Just what I need," he muttered to himself. "Lookin' like a teenager asking for a ticket and right in front of the cop station."

He found a parking spot under a tree. Looking around, he saw that no one seemed to be watching him or had taken notice of his work on the road. *Must happen all the time. Got lucky, too, to find a shady spot. Hope the birds are nesting elsewhere.*

He walked to the building, and as he neared, he heard the buzzer on the secure door sound. The door shuttered a mite. Roger grabbed the handle and walked in.

"Well, hello, Mr. Pyles. It's good to see you today."

"Thanks, Charlotte for buzzing me in, but please call me

Roger. How are you today?"

"Right as rain, well almost, and that ain't so bad. Could be a lot worse."

"It could. How's the weather outside? I heard some thunder."

Roger said, "It was coming down like there was no tomorrow south of here, but it looks like the storm'll miss this area."

"Welcome to the Sunshine State," she said. "I got some good news today. My concealed permit arrived. I'm gonna celebrate at the gun range later. Want to come along and do some shooting, Roger?"

"Thanks for the offer. Maybe some other time. I see you have a gloomy picture on your des k today. So the early warning system for Agent Hernandez's mood reads gloomy today. You know she knows about the system, right."

"Yes, word got out, but I decided to keep the charade going. It seemed to amuse her. Don't tell her this, but we have a new system. Check out the picture behind me."

Roger looked at a tranquil mountain scene with some dark clouds on the horizon. "So that's the new one?"

"It is. Today she's kinda calm, but it seems like she's concerned about something coming."

"That's interesting. Thanks for the update. Any idea what the concern could be?"

"Your guess is as good as mine, Roger. She's a private person and doesn't share much with me. She politely says hello, and then I watch how she goes up the stairs. Some days, she's in a hurry. Other times, it's just a normal walk, and some days, it's more of a stomp. Today it was several shades of stomp, so that's the reason for the mountain picture behind me."

"Thanks, Charlotte for the new heads up. Is she in?"

"She is. Go on up. I know you'll be prepared."

"Okay. Wish me luck," he said.

"Good luck," she said. "You may need it."

Roger headed up the stairs and stopped at Agent Hernandez's office. The door was open, and he looked in. She saw him and motioned for him to come on in. "Be with you in a minute. Grab a coffee, and I be able to talk in a jiffy."

"Okay," he said. Roger found a Styrofoam cup, poured himself a cup, and took a sip. Ahh. Black and strong like he liked. He sat down and waited. She was busy with some paperwork; something he knew never seemed to end. After finishing off his first cup, he got a second and was nearly finished it when she said, "Finally done. Nothing like a morning of paperwork to make you want out of your office. Roger Pyles, good morning. I was thinking about you today. Glad you showed up. We have much to talk about."

Roger was a bit taken back, but recovered quickly. "That's good to know. How have you been since I last saw you?"

"Hungry."

"Yeah, hungry. I had a light breakfast, and now I'm hungry. Want to do lunch?"

"Sure," he said. "Where would you suggest?"

"Sonny's Bar-B-Q. They're close, the food's good, and prices are right. Are you game?"

"Sounds good to me."

"And it's my treat. How's that for an offer you can't refuse?"

"Sure. No strings attached?"

"Nope. No strings attached. Just you and me and a much-needed talk."

Roger said, "Well, what are we waiting for? Let's go."

"Okay." She got up from her chair and followed Roger out the office door that she closed. They walked down the stair, and she spoke to Charlotte, "Charlotte, we're going to lunch. I have some things I need to talk to Roger about. Let my calls go to the answering machine. We should be back in an hour or hour and a half."

"All right. You two enjoy yourselves."

Agent Hernandez smiled slightly. Roger noted this and wondered about it, but had no clear idea why she reacted as she did. They walked out to a Brevard County Deputy's car, one with a big light bar across the top. She opened the doors and said, "Get in."

"Wow, I get to ride in the front seat this time."

They got in, and she asked, "Front seat? How many times have you ridden in the back seat?"

"Oh, a few times."

"Under arrest or not?"

"Oh, something like that."

She gave him a suspicious look, and he said, "I could usually out run the cops when I needed too."

"I hope you're kidding about that."

"Yeah, I'm kidding." He looked at her but could tell she wasn't convinced, which pleased him. He suppressed a grin, trying to form on his face.

She rolled her eyes. "Roger, there's much I don't know about you."

"And much I also don't know about you. Step on it. I wasn't hungry till you mentioned lunch, and now I'm starved. Turn on the lights and siren and get them out of the way."

She smiled, "I can't do that." She paused, "Though I'd like to," and laughed.

"What good is a cop car if you can't use it?"

"Roger, you're bad. Are you trying to get me fired?"

His countenance changed. "No," he lamented. "I've been fired, and it was no fun. I wouldn't wish that on an enemy. Just get us there. My stomach is trying to eat my backbone."

"Will do."

The rest of the drive was uneventful. Roger noted how courteous people were driving around them. A police car could do that. They pulled into Sonny's parking lot and were soon inside sitting at a booth in the back. It was still early for lunch, and the restaurant had few customers who were all sitting in the front. They both ordered coffee. Roger headed for the bathroom. After taking care of business and washing his hands, he returned and found a waitress taking their orders. She left as Roger returned. Hernandez said, "Seeing as I'm paying, and you weren't here, I ordered for you."

"What am I having?" he asked.

"Same thing I am, a Sonny's Sampler. It's a little bit of everything. You can't go wrong with it."

"Sounds good. What's on your mind?"

She said, "You've been living an interesting life lately."

"Tell me about it." He took a sip of the black coffee.

"I heard some scuttlebutt about your truck having some interesting cargo."

Roger said, "Yeah, you could call two dead bodies interesting cargo. I just got the truck back from the impound yard in Rockledge. I think I still want to get it cleaned at a car wash even though I got caught in a downpour coming over here. God only knows what kind of

119

residues we'd find from the bodies and the processing the investigators did. I'd like to start out with it being fresh."

"I can understand that. I can imagine a lot of nasty still being in it. If I were you, I'd have it pressure washed with some industrial strength soap."

"Agreed. I stopped in at the coroner's office next door to the impound yard and got an earful. It seems I'm a low-level person of interest in the deaths of the two men, but for all practical matters, they've cleared me. The coroner filled me in on some details on the dead guys' cause of death, strangulation, and it was done by someone or someones who knew what they were doing. They probably died in my yard and then transported to my truck I left at the bar."

She asked, "Why did you leave your truck at the bar?"

Roger shifted a little uneasily. "I was drunk, and Bill Kenney came and took me home. I spent the night at his house when the show was playing out. Guess having Bill verify where I was, is why the cops haven't much interest in me as a suspect."

"Interesting," she said.

"The two guys were ID'ed from fingerprints on record. Those boys had rap sheets, nothing out of the usual for small-time criminals, but the severity of their crimes seemed to have been escalating. They had some ties to the rotting corpse recently found up behind Riverside Baptist Church. Yeah, it's been an interesting week. After three days of staying with Bill, I was fit to be tied. He's a good friend I've known for what seems forever, but he can drive you crazy."

"Sounds like marriage to me."

Roger rolled his eyes, "Oh, please. I needed to get away from him as much as he needed to get away from me."

"I can relate to that. At least you guys didn't get in a fight."

"I think we both thought of it, but what would it have solved?

120

We've all seen the troubles violence causes."

"Roger, I'm going to tell you a secret. When my marriage was falling apart, my husband and me got in an argument. He struck me across my face and knocked me down. I was so mad; I went for a gun. I aimed it at him and pulled the trigger. Lucky for us, there wasn't a round in the chamber. I shudder to think what would have happened if I'd shot him."

"Were you aiming to kill?"

"What do you think?"

Roger said, "I see."

There was a moment of silence between them. A waitress carrying their meal walked up to them. "Here you go. Anything else I can get you?" She asked.

"Ketchup for the fries," Roger said.

"It's behind the roll of paper napkins," she said.

Roger shook his head and gave his best Sam Elliott imitation, "I must be blind."

The waitress smiled and put her finger to her lips. "You're not that movie star, are you? Now, what's his name? Are you Tom Selleck?"

Roger laughed, "No, first time I've been mistaken for him."

She said, "But you were the other guy in those cowboy movies."

"You're thinking of Sam Elliott, but I ain't him either, but I get mistaken for him often."

"No, you're him. Would you sign my order pad, please?"

"Sure," he said, and he did. She left happy.

Roger looked at Hernandez, who had been looking at him. "What?"

"What did you sign?"

"Sam Elliott, AKA Roger Pyles."

"You scoundrel."

Roger grinned, "Yeah, but I made her happy, didn't I?"

"You did. Does this happen all the time?"

"Yup. Back in the bad old days when I was wild and crazy, I had young women want to have sex with me because they thought I was him."

"And how did that end?"

He grinned, "I'll never tell."

"I see. I think we need to quit talking for now and eat before the food gets cold. It sure smells good."

"It does. Let's eat." And they did, heartily.

There was little small talk between them as they ate. Roger asked for several kinds of BBQ sauce that sat close to Hernandez. He found he liked the sweet version best. She needed additional paper towels to clean the tasty sauce from her mouth and fingers. She especially liked the sticky baby backed ribs. Roger pulled a toothpick from a shirt pocket and said, "You mind if I work on a piece of meat stuck between my teeth?"

"No," she said. "Got another toothpick, a clean one? I have a similar problem?"

He reached into his pocket and produced one still in the protective wrapper. "Here you go."

"Thanks." They both worked at the task. She had more success than he did.

The waitress came and asked, "Anything else?"

Gloria Hernandez said, "A box. I couldn't eat all this, and it's too good to throw away. And the check. My treat, Roger."

He looked surprised. "You don't have to do that, you know."

"I know, but I want to," Hernandez said. "And I'll not take no for an answer."

"Okay," he said. "I know a man can never win an argument with a woman, so thanks."

"You're welcome," she said.

The waitress said, "I'll be right back," and she was. The lunch crowd had just walked in the door. She handed the bill and black Styrofoam box to the policewoman.

"Great meal," Hernandez said to the waitress who smiled.

She said, "We aim to please. Thanks. You guys have a great day," and left quickly.

Roger watched as Gloria Hernandez shifted uneasily in her seat. "Thanks for lunch. You didn't have too, really."

"I wanted to."

"Thanks again." He looked her in the eye. "Now, what was it you wanted to talk to me about?"

"Was it that obvious?"

He said, "I had a feeling you had an ulterior motive to get me away from the county building and someplace where we could talk. What's on your mind?"

She inhaled deeply and let it out. "Roger, I did something I shouldn't have, and it involved you." She stopped, and the silence between them was deafening.

After a long moment, he said, "Go on." His face had a flat expression.

"I've suspected something for a long time." She stopped again, and Roger waited for her to continue. "I took some liberties with you. I got one of the coffee cups you used from the trash can some time ago."

"Go on."

"At my own expense, not the county's dime, I sent the DNA sample you left on it off to a laboratory. It wasn't cheap." She felt like his eyes were staring right through her. "And I sent my son's DNA sample in too for a comparison." Roger remained silent. "And it came back positive. That little fling we had in Las Vegas years ago where I first met you at the forensic convention, well, we made a baby. We have a child together, a 6-year-old boy." Roger remained quiet. "Aren't you going to say something, Roger?"

He put his hand to his mouth and chin. "It's a surprise all right, as least I suspected."

There was shock on her face and in her voice, "You knew? How? I was expecting this to be a bombshell moment."

"That thought crossed my mind some time ago, but I shrugged it off. It didn't seem possible, but it kept coming up in my head. When I sat in your office today, I was almost sure of it. You had a picture of him on your desk, something you didn't have before, and I got a good look at it. My mom had pictures of our family taken every year. When I saw the picture of your son, I was looking at a near replica of myself at that age, and you just confirmed what I already thought could be. What surprised me was they can do that with DNA now."

"Guess I should have known. You're good at seeing through the fog and figuring out what's going on. DNA paternity is not available at this time to the general public, but if you know where to look, it can be done."

"I think we'll be hearing a lot about this DNA thing in the future," he said. "So, where's that leave us now?"

"I don't know. I wasn't sure how you'd react to the news."

"Let's just say I'm a little shocked and in disbelief," Roger said. "I lost my whole family two years ago, and it seemed like I lost everything at that time, and now I find I'm not alone in this world. How would you think I should feel?"

She said, "I'd say you were taking it fairly well, considering."

"Again, where's that leave us now?"

"I don't know. Guess we'll have to work it through."

He nodded. "Do you want or need child support?"

"No. My son, our son's birth certificate has my ex-husband's name listed as his father. I never wanted child support from him, and he's out of the picture and my life. Roger, I'm not sure what I want or expect at this time. I'm sorry I did what I did. I had to know. Do you understand?"

"Yes."

"Do you hold it against me?"

"No," he said. "Under similar circumstances, I probably would have done the same. As I said, we'll have to work this through. It's not a life or death situation. I would say we keep this between ourselves for the foreseeable future and maybe then some. These are uncharted waters for me."

"Agreed. He's my son, my only living relative in the world. We'll play this one by ear."

Roger nodded. "Yeah, he's my son too. This place is starting to get busy, and our conversation won't be private much longer. Let's talk about this matter sometime in the future. We'll work something out."

"Good idea and duty calls for me. I need to get back at the office."

"Thanks for lunch. It's been one I won't forget."

She smiled knowingly, "You're welcome."

They got up, and she paid the bill. Neither spoke on the ride back to the office. Each seemed lost in their thoughts. From the corner of his eye, Roger caught her looking at him with questions in her eyes. He knew he had some of the same questions running through his head. They hit the lights right and arrived at the county office building. Both got out. They walked over to Roger's truck. Neither seemed to know what to say. After a moment, Roger said, "I'll be in touch. Bye."

"Okay, bye."

He backed the truck out and pulled to the main street. Luck was with him, and he was able to pull right out. Roger looked over his shoulder cautiously and saw Hernandez standing watching him go. He hoped she hadn't seen him look, but part of him wanted her to know he had. Life could sure get complicated, but what else was new? He wondered what other surprises awaited him.

# Chapter 25

"No, stop it. No more. I can't take no more of this. Stop kissing me." But the wet, gushy kissing continued and increased on Roger's face. "Woman, I said, **stop it**!" Roger opened his eyes and looked into the eyes of the female who was smothering his face with kisses, doggie kisses. "K9, what are you doing?" he asked as she continued to lick his face as he lay in his La-Z-Boy chair on the screened-in porch.

Then he remembered the dream he had been having, a rather passionate dream. "Girl," he said, "You're kissin' good, but nothing like I was experiencing. You settle down. I love you, but you're not the same."

She looked at him with her big concerned eyes questioning. "K9, now you know there'll never be a replacement for you." This seemed to satisfy her. She yelped, and Roger stroked her head. "Good girl. Good ole K9. Always there when I need you. After a few moments of petting, she seemed contented and walked to her food bowl, took a bite, and then lay down. Her eyes closed, and she was soon snoring lightly. "Wish I could do that," Roger said under his breath.

He thought for a moment. Who was that woman he'd been with in his dream? She seemed vaguely familiar, but try as he might, he couldn't put a name to the blurry face. Perhaps it would come to him. He thought about his dream. He hadn't had a dream like that since he was single, and he was single again, but this was the first time since his wife's death he'd had an erotic dream, even if this one had been interrupted near the end. He wondered if he was ready for any relationship with a woman yet. As he pondered this thought, a car drove up and stopped in front of his trailer. The window rolled down, and K9 rose up and growled. "Roger Pyles?"

"Who wants to know?"

"It is you, Roger. I'd know a voice like that anywhere."

Roger looked at the car with a mixture of curiosity and suspicion. "Well, you have me at a disadvantage. Who am I speaking with?"

"Roger, don't you know me? Tim Mace."

"Who?"

"Tim Mace. I worked with you at the college in Maryland."

A knowing grin came to Roger's face. "Well, knock me over with a feather. What are you doing here? Give me a minute. I'll get the gate, and you can drive in."

"Sure thing."

K9 growled. "It's okay, girl. Tim's an old friend from way back. He's good people. You can trust him. No more growlin' and bitin'. You can save that for Bill, though I wouldn't bite him. He'd leave a bad taste in your mouth."

That seemed to satisfy her. Roger opened the door and walked to the gate with K9 following along. He opened the gate, and Tim drove in and stopped. Roger left the gate open and walked to the car. Tim was out of the car and standing with his hand extended. Roger shook it, and the two men chest bumped. After more glad-handing and back-slapping, Roger asked. "What brings you to this woebegone part of the earth, Tim?"

"A bunch of things too numerous to talk about in the sun. How about we continue this conversation on your porch or in the trailer?"

"My porch is where I meet friends. Trailer ain't much inside, but this is home. Hey, you want a beer?"

"Sure, just like old times. Where do I park my car?"

"Anywhere over there." Roger pointed to a place next to his truck. "Meet me on the porch. Would a Yuenglings hit the spot?"

"Sure. Good old Pennsylvania beer. How do you get it here?"

Roger smiled, "I have my sources."

"That's the Roger I know. Making things happen."

Roger smiled. "No secret. A local place gets it. I don't know their supplier, but why look a gift horse in the mouth?"

"Or the beer mug."

"Or the mug," Roger repeated.

Tim got into his car and drove to the place Roger had designated. Roger handed him a twelve-ounce can as he entered the porch door. K9 sniffed Tim's leg. He allowed her to smell his hand also, which she did. She then lay down near her food bowl.

Roger said, "Looks like you passed inspection. The La-Z-Boy is mine. Take the other seat. It's comfortable too."

"Will do." The men sat down, and the sound of two pop-top cans opening was heard. "Ah," Tim said. "Good to the last drop."

"It is, but isn't that about coffee?"

"It is," Tim said. "That's my newest vice."

"Really? Mine too. I never took you to be a coffee drinker."

"Roger, some things never change, but some do." He looked at the La-Z-Boy. "Nice chair. Looks new."

"It is. The last one got shot up with me almost in it."

Surprise showed on Tim's face. "What happened? Jealous husband after you or maybe one of those or-something?"

"No, nothing as exciting as a jealous husband. I haven't had much interest in women since my wife died."

"She was a good woman. You married up with Kay. I only met her once, but she left a good impression on me."

Roger nodded, "She did that with most everyone. I know I married up. Don't know if I'll ever find another one like her in a million years. Think they broke the mold when they made her."

"I can tell you still miss her."

"Don't know if I'll ever get over losing her."

Tim said. "This little town is sure, shall we say, interesting."

"That's an understatement."

"I drove by the little store on the way in and there was a crowd of people all standing around trying to look at something around the side of the building."

"That would be Miller's Store run by an old woman and her autistic son, Fred. Can't say I ever saw a crowd there before. Not that many people in this little town. What was going on?"

Tim said, "I was curious about that too, so I stopped to see too. I worked my way through the crowd. Some cop was trying to keep order."

"That would be Bill Kenney, our one-man police force and the closest thing I've got to a friend in this world. What was the commotion about?"

"A bear was cornered by a fence outside the store."

"A bear?"

"Yeah, a bear. A young bear. One of the locals said they were waiting for the wildlife people to come and get him."

"Bears are normally found many miles west of the St. Johns River. Can't say I ever heard of one here ever."

"The man said the same. He speculated the youngin' was recently separated from his momma and wasn't taking the change too well."

"Yeah, sometimes that happens, and they take off in a hurry often going nowhere. Sounds like this little boy got himself lost and in a heap of trouble."

Tim said, "I agree. My curiosity satisfied, I left and came here."

"I see." Roger stopped. "It was an or-something."

"Come again?"

Roger said, "The or-something was a local murder investigation I was helping out on. The bad guys didn't like that I was getting close to the killer and tried to eliminate me. If K9 hadn't alerted me, I'd been pushing up daisies now."

"Wow. That's quite a story."

"You got the abridged version."

"What's the full story?" Tim asked.

"Maybe another time. What's new with you? It's been a goodly time since I've swapped lies with you. Still single? Still working at our old college?"

Tim exhaled deeply. "So much has changed, and so much remains the same. It's hard to know where to start."

"How about since I last saw you up north?"

Tim took a sip of the cold beer. "Ah, nothing like a cold beer to hit the spot on a hot day in Florida." He paused. "So you want the whole story?"

"Just the facts as they liked to say on the old Dragnet TV series. Just the facts, Tim."

"Okay, you remember I was one of the few professors at the college who stood up for you and academic freedom."

"I do, and I'm grateful for that. It took courage to stand against the other faculty gunning for me. Thanks. How did it work out for you?"

"They came gunning for me and some others after you left. It was a very hostile environment on campus, and we either resigned or took other positions when our contract was up. This created a real uproar at the school, especially with the alumni. Contributions from them dropped off significantly, and all the hoopla caught the eye of some government officials who felt some discrimination laws could have been broken. The president of the school and some other high-up in the administration resigned, and things have settled down somewhat."

Roger said, "I'm sorry your decision cost you your job."

"Don't be. It all worked out for me. Life has a way of doing that if you wait. Sometimes, the wait is short. Other times, it can take a while, a decade, or longer."

Roger sighed, "I'm still working through the working it out stage. I'm glad to hear yours was short. What happened?"

"I took a position at Waynesburg University and couldn't be happier."

"Waynesburg? That's a surprise. What's an atheist like you doing teaching at a Christian school?"

"I've moved up a notch on my beliefs. I'm now an agnostic. I've moved to the point where I willing to entertain the idea of there being some outside source responsible for the existence of the universe. I'm still working my way through this journey."

"That's a big surprise."

Tim said, "There was just too much evidence I couldn't ignore."

"So how'd you get on at a Presbyterian school?"

"A guy I went to undergrad school was teaching there. We kept in touch after graduation. I hadn't heard from him in years and out of the blue, he calls me up, said he was thinkin' about me, asked what I'm doin', I tell him, and he asks me if I'm interested in another job. I said yes, they interview me, and then hired me."

"So your being an atheist wasn't a problem, Tim?"

"Agnostic. I'm now willing to admit I'm not sure and don't know it all. It was a big step for me. There could be something more out there. The college people asked if I could be fair and present both sides. I said yes, and they hired me."

"So what's it been like?"

"Honestly Roger, they've treated me fine. I've had more academic freedom at the church school than I did at the state school."

"That's great it worked out for you." He stopped. "So what brings you to Florida? Mickey Mouse?"

Tim smiled, "I thought I might go over to Orlando and see the Magic Kingdom and maybe even that new place EPCOT while here, but I had several other things on my mind."

"And they are?"

"A local college is looking for someone with my qualifications."

Roger said, "But wait. There's more. I can tell. Spill the beans."

"I heard you had, shall we say, some difficulties lately and you may need some professional help."

Roger gave his best Sam Elliott laugh. "Professional help? Ain't that a hoot. What kind of professional help do you, of all people, have to offer?"

"This kind." He lifted his shirt to reveal a sleek handgun.

Roger whistled through his teeth. "That's one fancy gun. Can't say I ever saw one like that. What is it?"

"It's a Glock 17, Austrian made. Not many in the US yet."

"How'd you get it?"

"I'd tell you, but I'd have to kill you."

"Never mind. I didn't want to know that bad." He smiled. "Tim, from what you've said, there seems to be much I don't know about you.'

Tim smiled but said nothing.

Roger rubbed his chin. "Considering the fact I seem to have a bullseye painted on me, I could use some protection. What's it gonna cost me?"

"Nothing."

"Nothing?"

"That's right. Nothing. I could use a place to stay for a while until I need to return back up north."

"Well, you're welcome here, that's for sure. Why no charge?"

"A favor to you."

"A favor to me? What did I do to deserve this?" Roger asked.

Tim was about to speak, but Roger cut him off. "Let me guess. You could tell me, but you'd have to kill me. Right?"

"You get the picture. Best you don't ask too many questions."

Roger looked at him suspiciously. "I'm glad I trust you."

Tim smiled. "We'll work out the details as we go along. You won't even know I'm here."

"Right. I'm not so sure I like this idea, but I think it's for the best."

Tim nodded. "Right."

A truck pulling a horse hauler appeared on Canaveral Flats Boulevard and turned left onto the country lane down to Roger's trailer. Tim looked at Roger. "You expecting anyone?"

"No, but I think I know the owner of the truck. Not sure why he's got the horse trailer, though."

Bill Kenney got out of the truck. "Roger Pyles. Just the person I wanted to see. I hope I'm not interrupting anything important."

"Nothing that can't wait. Come on in and take a load off. What's on your little pea picking mind?" Bill walked into the trailer porch. "Want a beer?"

He smiled, "I do, but I'm on duty."

Roger could tell Bill wasn't too sure of his guest. "Bill, this is my friend, Tim Mace. We knew each other from back up north. He's had my back several times in the past."

"Pleased to meet you, Mr. Mace."

"It's Tim. Should I call you by your first name or something more formal, Officer?"

"Bill's fine. We're not very formal around here. What brings you to Florida, Tim?"

"Business and pleasure."

"That sounds like most of our visitors. Spend lots of money and keep my taxes low, please."

The men laughed. Roger said, "So what brings you here, Bill? Tim tells me you had some excitement at the store. How did it work out?"

"I thought you looked familiar, Tim. You were with the looky-loos at Millers."

"I was. How did it go for the bear?"

"The wildlife people arrived just after you left, shot him with a tranquilizer dart, and he was down for the count. They put him in a special bear cage they brought along, so I guess he's gonna be checked out and then released somewhere in the Ocala National Forest. They said they woulda been here quicker, but all the bear cages were north of Orlando where the problems normally are. I think that's the last we'll see of Yogi."

Roger said, "Yogi? Who named him that?"

Bill said, "Some little boy. Think it was the Riggan's Kid. He's got quite an imagination."

"So what's on your mind, Bill? What brings you to my humble abode this day?"

"I have a favor to ask of you. Come with me." The two men followed Bill out the door and to the trailer. They looked in. "It's a mule," Roger said.

Bill said, "Close but no cigar. He's a donkey."

"Where'd you get him?" Roger asked.

"I got a call about a hurt animal in the road, and this is what I found."

Roger looked more closely at the creature. "He's got some cuts on him. What do you think happened?"

"My guess is he's been abandoned by someone and had a rough time with some barbed wire fences. He's a little underweight, looks malnourished. I checked around, and no one seems to be missing a donkey. I hate it when people dump off animals."

"Me too, but what's he got to do with me if anything?"

"Well, Roger. He needs a temporary place to stay until he finds a home. You got five acres that need mowing. There's always water in the ditch in the back. He'd be no trouble. You have a lean-to he could use for shelter from storms and some trees for shade."

"Storms? Yeah, I've noted this state definitely has some storms, hurricanes, afternoon thunderstorms. Yup, Florida does have some serious storms, Bill."

"And don't forget hailstorms."

"Hailstorms? Are you kidding?"

"No. Last year nearby Altamonte Springs had a big hailstorm. Hail was a couple of inches deep on the ground. In some car lots along Semoran Boulevard near the mall, every vehicle suffered damage. They looked like a bunch of little kids had gotten loose with ball peen hammers and put dings and dents all over them."

Roger said, "Definitely need some shelter. Bill, he's looking pretty cut up."

Tim spoke up, "I've had some experience in dressing wounds. His look bad, but I don't see any that need stitches. Cleaning and putting some antiseptics on them would do wonders for him. Does he have a name?"

"Nope. No name. No home. No one to care for him."

Roger said, "Doesn't the county have an animal farm or something like that for foundlings like him?"

"I checked. They're full and overflowing. Can't take him. They told me to take care of the situation best I could. They suggested it might be best if I put him down and be done with it."

Roger shook his head. "So, he's got no name, no home, and no hope?"

"That pretty much sums it up. I'm out of options, Roger."

He said nothing for a moment and appeared to be thinking. "Okay, I'll take him, but only till he finds a good home. I don't know much about caring for a critter like him."

Tim said, "I'll help you. Let's get started. I'll shut the gate, so he doesn't get out."

As they waited for the gate closing, Bill got something from the cab, carrots. Roger said, "I should have known, the carrot or the stick."

"You got it. I tried to pull him into the horse trailer. Then I tried to push him in with no success. It would've been comical if it hadn't been me trying to do it. He went right in when I put carrots in the trailer. Guess he was hungry." Bill gave Roger the carrots. "You'll need these."

"Got the gate closed," yelled Tim.

Bill opened the door on the horse trailer and waited, but the donkey did not move from the trailer. "Feed him a carrot, Roger."

135

Roger held a carrot in front of the donkey. He looked at it with a mixture of suspicion and curiosity. After a moment of hesitation, he reached forward, opened his mouth and took it with his teeth and lips. It was soon gone, and he looked for more. Roger backed up and held out another. To reach it, the donkey had to stick his head out of the door which he did and took the carrot.

"So far, so good," Roger said. He dropped several carrots on the ground ten feet from the trailer. The donkey looked at them and then at the men. "It's okay, donkey with no name. We won't hurt you here. You can trust us."

The donkey hesitated, swung his head from side to side, and looked around. He stepped out. Apparently, he liked what he saw. Bill shut the door to the horse trailer and said, "Well, Roger, looks like you've got a guest for a while."

Roger wondered if he meant the donkey or Tim or both. "Yeah, guess I do." *What've I got myself into this time?*

# Chapter 26

One week later

"I can't believe the change in that donkey. He came in here, frightened and suspicious of everyone, and you changed him, Tim. The way you worked at healing that donkey could best be described as mystical."

"I've been told that before. When I was on assignment, I worked with horses and donkeys a lot. One guy called me a 'Whisperer' of all things. I have a way with them, but I think it's just patience and showing them kindness. Did you know donkeys are indispensable in Third World countries? People ride them. They're the tractors used to till the soil. They serve, and people there can't do without them."

"I remember seeing them doing that when I was overseas, but I never thought about it."

"Yup, I guess a donkey was the original service animal."

"That and a dog."

"True. K9 and the no-name donkey don't seem to get along very well."

Tim said, "That goes back a long time. Dogs and wolves were the enemies of donkeys, and I suspect the donkey with no name had some ugly encounters with some dogs lately. Some of those cuts could have been bites. Give it time. They'll learn to tolerate each other and maybe even eventually accept each other."

"Could be. We can hope. The donkey had no problem with my cat."

"Not natural enemies and both have a big streak of curiosity,' Tim mused, "You can find stories about donkeys everywhere. The Persians have an ancient tale called 'The Fool and the Donkey.' The Brothers Grimm have fairy tales about donkeys. You know the story about the farmer whose old donkey fell in an old dry well?"

"I do. The farmer dumped dirt in the well to bury the animal, but the beast stepped on the ever-rising dirt dumped in the well and used it to escape."

"And let's not forget the story of Balaam and his talking donkey in the Bible."

Roger laughed, "Talking donkeys? Reminds me of some politicians."

Tim said, "I didn't mean to get political, but if the shoe fits..."

The men both laughed.

"So where were you when you learned so much about donkeys?" Roger asked.

Tim gave him a dirty look.

"So let me guess. If you told me, you'd have to kill me?"

Tim shook his head. "It's not that serious, but there are some things I'd rather not go into. It might be best if you didn't know. Do you think you know how to treat his wounds?"

"I think I can manage, but I don't know if I can get him to trust me like you do."

Tim said, "It just takes time and patience. Show them you can be trusted, and before long, you'll have a big pet and friend."

"Maybe he'll have found a real home by then."

Tim gave Roger a knowing look, but said nothing for a moment. "It's been an interesting week."

"It has. It was great to catch up on old times with the stories you could share. You gave me a new one, you know?"

"And what would that be?"

Surprised, Roger said, "Why the way you corralled those horses that got loose and were running around town. You got them to come on my property and how they roamed the place till we could find the owner, old man Dennison who lives in the back of this little Podunk town."

"It was easy for me. As you indicated, I speak fluent Equestrian. Donkey sure liked it during the time the two geldings and young mare were here. He thought he was one of them even with his crazy braying. He's walked with more confidence since then. He sure liked the mare."

"I've noticed that too. He seemed sad to see them go. Speaking of the donkey, where is he?"

"I don't know. He did seem a little moody since his friends left. Maybe he's over in the trees by the edge of the property with the neighbor's cow."

"Could be. I guess the company of a cow is better than none."

"Yeah, I guess so. You know, donkeys aren't dumb and stubborn creatures like some people think. They hesitate doing things that are new, and they don't understand."

Roger said, "So I'm learning."

"You can learn a lot from a donkey if you just listen and have patience."

Roger nodded. "So I'm discovering. We can find wisdom from the most unlikely of sources."

Tim grinned and gave Roger another knowing look, "So I'm learning," he said slowly drawing out the phrase.

Roger grunted, "I think I've been insulted, but what are friends for?"

"Yeah, Roger. One last bit of advice."

"What's that?"

"Try to stay upwind as much as possible. Donkey farts are killers."

"Like ogres?"

"Ogres are said to fart a lot. Don't know about the smell. Now this donkey, he farts a lot, and they're bad."

Roger said, "That's worth remembering."

"Old buddy, I've been staying with you for a week, and it seemed like your donkey needs me as much as you needed me to see trouble didn't come your way. I think it's time for me to find other quarters. You know what they say. Guests and fish start to smell after three days, and I've more than doubled that amount."

"You don't have to go. It was kind of nice to have another warm body around the place."

"You have a cat, a dog, and a donkey."

"They all shed, and the conversations are kinda one-sided."

"True," Tim said. "But I need to be moving on. You know how to take care of the donkey now, and no one is going to sneak up on this place with him around. Whenever someone shows up, his braying could wake the dead."

"It would, but what if I need some firepower? I know a little about firearms, but I'm not proficient with them."

"I think you'll be alright. Why don't you take a class from the local sheriff's department, or the NRA, or some group like that so you'll feel safer?"

"Guess I could. Doing this investigative work may make it necessary."

"You don't have to become an expert, just comfortable with them, competent."

"So I wouldn't shoot myself?"

"That's the idea."

"That would be embarrassing."

"And painful."

Roger nodded. "Looks like I got another thing on my To-Do list. When are you leaving?"

"Now."

"So soon?"

"Yeah, duty calls and I must answer. I'll grab my things to go. What do I own you for your hospitality? I want to give you something."

"Tim, you're no problem. I enjoyed the company and your help with Mr. Donkey. And I felt a lot safer with you around. You sure you got to go?"

"It's for the best. It will be alright here, I'm sure."

"Well, if you're sure."

Tim got up from the chair and walked in the trailer. He wasn't in it very long and emerged with a small suitcase. He put it in his vehicle and walked to Roger. He said, "Old buddy, it was good to see you and glad I could help. You take care, and if you need me, you know how to contact me."

"Thanks. I appreciate your help and hope it works out for you too." He stuck out his hand, and Tim shook it, then pulled him close and shoulder bumped him.

Tim said, "Take care of yourself."

"I will."

Tim got to his car and drove to the gate. Roger opened it for him. As Tim was leaving, he stopped and said to his friend, "Oh, I think I might know where your donkey is."

"Yeah? Where?"

"Someplace other than here. While I was in the trailer, I happened to look out the back window. There's a donkey sized hole in your back fence."

"Oh, no. Looks like he's on the run. I better call Bill and let him know he's on the loose again."

"Got to go Rog. You know where to find me. See yah."

Roger waved as Tim drove off. He soon disappeared. Roger let out a sigh. *Where was that donkey?* He was beginning to like him. As Roger pondered the question, a car approached, a Honda Civic. It stopped in front of him. "Hello, Roger. Got a few minutes?"

"Sure, Pastor Nassey. I can make time for you. Come on down to the trailer. Do you know anything about fixing a fence?"

"Sure do. Fixed a bunch in my time."

The Pastor drove in and parked his car. The two men found some tools and barbed wire in the lean-to. It didn't take long for the patch to be applied. Roger thanked the Pastor for his help and told him to help himself to a drink of his choice from the refrigerator while he put the tools back. When he came back, he found the Pastor with a beer and a bottle of ice tea in front of him. "Tea for me and a beer for you, Pastor?"

"Nah, I swore off beer a long time ago. Seems like alcohol got me in a whole lot of trouble. I'll take the tea, thanks."

"I think I'll get tea too." Roger took the beer back to the refrigerator and returned with a bottle of ice tea. "What's on your mind, Pastor?"

He began to speak, "I'm not sure how to start this, but it goes something like this: I was down at the church the other day and ..." He stopped as a truck with its emergency lights flashing pulled slowly from Canaveral Flats Boulevard into Roger's driveway. It was Chief of Police Bill Kenney and a tethered donkey plotted along behind the truck. Roger recognized the second truck, and it belonged to old man Dennison, owner of the horses who had come to visit recently, and he appeared to be somewhat under the influence.

141

The Pastor looked at Roger for an explanation who shrugged his shoulders. The men got up and walked out to the two men who were now out of their trucks. Bill said to Roger, "We have a donkey problem."

"Uh-oh. What happened?"

Old man Dennison began to speak, "That donkey of yurs," he mumbled. "He found his way to my place and got to my mare. I was keepin' her away from the studs, and that sad, sorry critter got to her. He had his way with her he did. It took me a while to find them in the woods and figure what was goin' on. They was like, layin' down there, smokin' cigarettes after the dirty deed was done."

Roger couldn't believe what he was hearing. The words, "He's not my donkey," blurted from his mouth. "I'm just keeping him as a favor to Bill."

Chief of Police Bill Kenney gave Roger a stare that could sour milk.

"What are you gonna do about this?" the man slurred.

Roger was silent for a moment. "At this point, I don't believe there's much we can do. Maybe, we need to wait and see if anything comes from the union of these two."

Old man Dennison staggered a bit. He raised his hand and tried to point at the Roger who appeared to be wavering as was his finger. He lowered it and said, "Yeah, don't think there's much we can do. We wait and hope for the best." He got in his truck and drove off.

Bill growled at Roger, "Thanks for spreading the guilt around, old buddy."

"But he's not my donkey. I'm just keeping him as a favor to you, remember, old buddy."

"Boys," said the Pastor. "No need to fight. The damage has been done and it looks like you got off easy. The donkey is back, and maybe there won't be a foal. How 'bout we settle down and check out the donkey. See if he's okay."

Bill said, "He's okay. Got some new cuts on his chest. They didn't look too bad."

"Probably where he went through the fence. I've done some dumb things too looking for love." The Pastor looked at Roger, and

Bill's face scrunched up as Roger realized his faux pas. "But it was a long time ago, and I've matured so much since then."

The Pastor let the comment slide. "Enough about love-struck donkeys. I'm glad you showed up. Bill, I've something I need to talk with you guys about."

"What is it?" Roger said.

"How about we close the gate, so he don't get out and get in any more trouble and then we dress his wounds?" Pastor said.

"Sounds like a plan," Bill said. He closed the gate. Roger got the medicine to dress the new cuts. It went quickly. All wounds were superficial, but the dried blood had made them look worse. Roger released the donkey, who he gave a nonchalant look to the men, pooped, and moseyed off nibbling at grass and weeds as if he didn't have a care in the world. The men went to the porch. Bill saw the two teas and got one for himself from the refrigerator. Roger found a chair for the new arrival, and they sat down and sipped at their teas. Roger said, "Okay, Pastor, what was so important that you had to drive out here to tell me, and now Bill?"

# Chapter 27

Pastor Nassey took a big swig of the iced tea and swallowed it. "Ah, I needed that. Guys, there's been some developments I think I need to speak about with you. As you know, I was involved with law enforcement in this county for decades before I became a pastor, so you can imagine I still have a lot of contacts and connections here. And I would like most of them to remain nameless. Also, I'm still a reserve officer in the force, and I see a lot of people I used to work with out on the highways and byways of Brevard County.

"Well, there's always been a drainage problem at the church down by the river near the amphitheater. A spring or seep had kept that area closest to the Indian River wet and soupy. As you can image, it's worse in the rainy season when we need to mow the area. At last month's deacons meeting, the subject came up again. The problem had always been they were afraid of what it would cost to fix this minor annoying problem. A new fellow at the church attended the Easter services, saw the problem, and volunteered to fix the problem for free. He had a backhoe and knew how to install a drainage pipe.

"Anyway, the deacons approved him doing it. I'm not sure if he was doing this out of the goodness of his heart, or he wanted to drum up some business. In all fairness, it could have been both. Last Saturday, he started to work on the project. He dug the ditch to the river. It was no problem in the soft sand and muck. When he got up near the seep, he dug up something, a rusted to pieces old box. The box wasn't the important thing, but what was falling out of it, jewels. Guys, I know about the body found down there having an emerald in his belly, and I know about the recent robbery at the Treasure Museum in Cape Canaveral, and I know about all the old stories and legends about the lost dowry containing the Queen's Jewels from the 1715 Spanish Fleet that sank in the hurricane. Guys, I think the backhoe operator discovered some. He stopped when he found it and notified me. I'm not sure if this is a blessing or not. The church sure could use the money. The roof's leaking, and we don't have the money to fix it properly, but I'm not sure we need the trouble this could have for us, if you know what I mean."

Roger said, "Yeah, I know what you mean. Seems like where there's treasure or gold, someone dies and it would seem some recent deaths and burglaries could be related to this, and probably are. What did you do with what you've found so far, Pastor?"

"It's in a safe deposit box at a local bank for the time being."

"What did you find so far?" Bill asked.

"Jewelry, gold and silver, mostly gold and the pieces had gemstones of many kinds and colors in them. I'm no expert on this, but my guess is the little stash we've found could pay for the needed roof many, many times over."

Roger said, "If those are the Queen's Jewels, they could be priceless." Bill nodded in agreement. Roger continued, "You said he stopped digging when he found the stuff. What's the status of the dig site now, Pastor?"

"He covered it up with some dirt. If anyone were to ask why he stopped, the cover story is he had business elsewhere demanding his attention. Honestly, I don't think there's that much more there, but you can never know for sure till you dig and see."

"You say the backhoe operator was new to the church," Bill said. "Can he be trusted, Pastor?"

"I believe so. He seems like an honest man and runs his business with Biblical principles. I checked with the local Better Business Bureau for a rating and complaints. He had the best they give and only a few grievances he did try to resolve, most successfully."

Roger said, "No, you can't please everyone, no matter how hard you try."

"Ain't that the truth?" Bill said.

"Not even as a pastor. Sometimes no good deed goes unpunished."

"Yup," Roger and Bill said almost in unison.

"So, what now, Pastor Phil?" Roger asked. "What are you gonna do now?"

"That's where I'm hoping you two come in." They shot him a questioning look. The pastor continued, "I need someone I can trust and someone with a little firepower backup if necessary. I'd like you two to dig up the site by hand with shovels. A backhoe could damage anything remaining to find. I know it'll be hard work. I was hoping for your help. I'll see you're compensated."

Roger said, "Compensation or none, I'm in."

"Me too," Bill said. "You can count on me."

"Good. Can you do it ASAP?"

Bill said, "I got tomorrow off. What're your plans for tomorrow, Roger?"

"Funny you should ask. I'll be at a certain dig too."

"That's good, guys. Start as early as you can, and you'll avoid some of the heat. I appreciate it."

They sipped at the tea. Each man seemed lost in his thoughts. After some time, Pastor asked, "Roger, how long have you had a donkey?"

"He's been here for about a week now. I don't know how much longer. It seems he can be a pain at times."

"Can't we all?" the pastor said. "You know, you can learn a lot from a donkey."

Roger said, "I seem to remember hearing that just today."

"That's interesting," the pastor replied. "I once read a book about the wisdom of donkeys. Wake up and have some quiet time. Plan your day. Have a good breakfast. Solve the problems you can. See the world for what it is. Scratch where it itches. Take time for others. Let them know you're here by doing something significant. Take a nap when tired. Solve any more problems you can. Poop regularly. Spend some time alone with nature and get a good night's sleep."

Roger said, "Yup, that about sums life up, especially the pooping part. Boy, oh boy, can some constipated people sure get grouchy."

The men laughed, and the pastor finished off his tea. "Guys, I hate to leave your pleasant company, but duty calls. I'll see you at the church tomorrow."

"Bill said, "We'll be there bright and early."

"That we will," Roger added.

"Bye, y'all."

They waved goodbye to the pastor. When his car was out of sight, Roger said to Bill, "How about a beer?"

"Sure thing. I love drinking **your** beer."

Roger got two beers. "What do you think we'll find tomorrow?"

"There are more things in heaven and earth, Horatio, than can be dreamed of."

"That's Hamlet. I didn't know you read Shakespeare, Bill."

"A little, but I saw it on a PBS show and to answer your question about what we'll find, that's a good question. And there's only one way to find out in any mystery case. We dig."

# Chapter 28

Shortly after daybreak, Bill picked up Roger at his trailer. The donkey brayed wildly when he arrived. The new alarm system was working well. After a short drive on Canaveral Flats Boulevard and US 1, Bill turned right at Riverside Baptist Church and saw a county deputy's car blocking the gate to the river by the Fellowship Building. As they approached it, a man got out, Deputy Yates. He waved for them to stop which they did.

"Yates, what are you doing here?" Bill Kenney hollered.

"I should have known. Whenever there's trouble, you'd show up. And you got Roger Pyles with you. Talk about double trouble."

"Hey, Yates. Good to see you again. What's going on? Pastor Nassey asked us to come over and do some work for him, and here you are."

"I'm finishing up my shift. I'm on nights this month and was working the area. It was quiet last night. I wrote a couple of speeding tickets on hot rodders who thought US 1 was the Daytona Speedway, but other than that, it was a typical night till I got the call about prowlers on the church property. I left my cruiser in the church parking lot and checked out the main church building and this side of the Fellowship Building. Nothing. Everything seemed normal, so I walked to the fence by the side of the fellowship hall, looked down to the river and saw lights that shouldn't have been there. I listened for a moment. I could make out two male voices, but wasn't able to tell what they were talking about though they seemed to be arguing.

"Anyway, I carefully slipped over the chain link fence without ripping the crotch of my pants out and hurting anything important."

Roger laughed, "Yeah, that would have been the talk of the whole department if you had hurt yourself there."

Deputy Yates shook his head. "It would, and I didn't want to be famous, so like I said, I was careful."

"You're so right," Bill said. "Years ago when I was doing union work with the Carpenters Union, I was on a big job in Orlando at Disney World. One of the night shift ironworkers, a welder, was doing work at one of the water parks. Some of the rebar rods holding up the lath and stucco of the fake rocks and boulders needed repair. He had to climb in this maze underneath, twist and turn till he got to the spot that needed attention. It was above his head. He had all his protective gear on, leathers and mask, but a piece of hot slag came off, went between his mask and the leathers protecting his shoulders. It got under his shirt. He was wiggling all around to try to get away from it without much success, and it only got worse. The hot slag piece got into his pants and stuck to the head of his favorite organ."

Yates and Roger both cringed. Bill continued the story, "The poor guy was in a lot of pain and was on workman's compensation until he healed up. They said the report on the incident circulated the whole of Disney World."

Roger said, "That sure would've put a crimp on his love life."

Yates said, "As I said, you don't want to be the safety topic of the month." He cleared his throat. "As I was saying, I listened for a while and decided to approach the men with my gun drawn. About halfway there, I tripped over something in the dark and fell, making a lot of noise. They heard it and made a run for the river. I yelled for them to stop, but they made a clean getaway in a boat. Lucky for me, I held on to the gun. I shined my light at where they disappeared, but they were gone.

"I checked out what they were doing, digging down by the river. I don't know what they were looking for, but I don't think they found anything. If they did, they took it with them. Say, what was it Pastor Nassey asked you to be here for?"

Bill said, "It involved the digging down at the river. Seems the backhoe operator stumbled onto something."

Yate's face took on a concerned look. "Let me guess. It wasn't an old rusty piece of machinery or space junk, but something valuable."

Roger said, "We think he may have found some of the Queen's Jewels from the 1715 Treasure Fleet."

Yates said, "Whoo, that would explain a lot on what's been going on around here. I hope he put whatever they found someplace safe."

Bill said, "It's in a safe place. He wanted us to do some digging and see if we could find anything else. He indicated he felt we wouldn't find much if anything, but he needed to be sure."

"Gotcha. Boys, I'm about to go off shift. I think you can take it from here. I'd see if those guys left any evidence. I never got a chance to look much. My flashlight died shortly after I started looking and the batteries were supposed to be new ones. I just replaced them. Guess I got some bad ones."

"It happens," Roger said. "Wonder how we're gonna get our truck down to the river?"

"Leave that to me," Bill said. "He went to the stairs leading to the second floor of the building and disappeared for a moment. "Voila." He held a key in his hand.

"Well, ain't you the smart one?" Yates said. "Looks like you boys are all set. I'm gonna head for the barn. You guys have a nice day and be careful. Seems like evil is all around and has many eyes."

Bill said, "We will. You have a good day." He gave the key to Roger. "You open the gate, and I'll drive my truck down to the river."

"Sounds like a plan. See yah, Yates."

"Righto. See you in the funny papers."

Roger opened the gate, and Bill drove through. Yate's cruiser stopped at US 1, made it halfway across and merged into southbound traffic. Roger walked down to the truck. "Bill, I think we need to approach this as a crime scene."

"Agreed. You bring a camera?"

"Of course. What kind of a doofus do you think I am?"

Bill smiled, "So you want me to answer that?"

Roger shot him a dirty look. "No. Sorry for asking. I should have known better considering the company I keep."

"No comment. You take some photo shots, and I'll look for anything the night time diggers may have left."

"Sounds like a plan. Let's get to work."

# Chapter 29

The two men looked over the dig area behind the church. Roger took pictures of how conditions were. Nothing seemed out of order. No tools, no jewels were lying in the dirt, not even a cigarette butt.

"What's you doin'?" said a small voice behind them.

The startled men looked at a young boy of about six. "What's you doin'?" he asked again.

"Where'd you come from?" Roger asked.

"Next door," the boy said. "Are you friends with the men who were here last night? I heard 'em talkin'. They woke me up, and I told my momma."

"Did she call the police about them?"

"I don't know." He shrugged his shoulders. "A cop showed up, and the men ran away. I don't think they were 'spose to be there."

"What's your name, boy?" Bill asked.

"George."

"George?"

"Yeah, Mom calls me Curious George, like the monkey."

"Curious George?" repeated Roger.

"Yeah. She says I'm just like him. Always curious. Always getting into trouble. I wish I was a monkey like George. I could climb trees with my hands and feet, and when I did get in trouble, they wouldn't make a big deal about it 'cause he's just a monkey."

Roger rubbed his chin. "Guess there are advantages to being a monkey."

"Yeah."

"Why aren't you getting ready for school today, George?"

"No school. Teacher's meeting. They got to work. I get to play. Yay."

"Where do you go to school?"

"I go to the church's school. It's a nice place. I like my teacher, Mrs. Massey. Do you know her?"

Roger said, "No, I don't think I do. Do you know her, Bill?"

"I think I've met her once. I wouldn't swear to it." He turned to George. "What are you doing up so early?"

"Mom and her boyfriend were making too much noise in her bedroom. They don't think I know what they're doing, but I do. I saw them one time. Mom and Dad are, separated, she called it. They used to fight over everything. Mom made more money, and my Dad didn't like it. He's not doing too well."

"Sorry to hear that, George. I hope they can work it out."

"Daddy has a bad temper. The cop who was here last night had to come to our house when they were fighting. That's how I knew him. He fell over a tricycle I left in the yard. I thought it was funny, but he didn't. He said some bad words when he fell and more when the bad guys got away."

"Why did you leave the tricycle out?"

He shrugged his shoulders. "Guess I forgot to put it away. I go to school here. Did I tell you that? I got it out of the playground."

Roger said, "I believe you did tell us that."

"Mom says I have monkey brains when I forget. I think it would still be good to be a monkey, monkey brains or not."

"Tell me George, what did you see last night? Why were you up?"

"I had to pee. When I went back to my room, I heard the men trying to be quiet and whisper. They had some lights and seemed to be digging."

"How many were there?" Bill asked.

"I only heard two voices. Could have been more. I don't know. I woke up Mom, and she called 911. Am I in trouble?"

"I don't think so George, but you need to stay away from the dig area. We need to investigate."

"Don't think you'll find much. It rained so hard; it woke me up. It was still dark. I had to close the window. It was coming in. I like to sleep with my window up." He pointed to a second-story window on the neighboring house. "That's my room up there. Did you know there's lots of noises at night? Lots of critters are up at night. Did you know that?"

Roger said, "Well, thank you for that bit of information. George, you've been very helpful, but I think you need to run along

152

now."

"Me too. My stomachs growling, and Mr. Big Ears needs to be fed."

Bill said, "Mr. Big Ears?"

"My bunny. I can tell him anything, and he listens. I like my bunny."

Bill smiled, "Yeah, It's good to have someone you can tell everything to."

"I can get some cereal and milk and berries for me if Mom's not up. Sometimes they stay in bed and make a lot of noise. I turn the TV on so I don't have to hear. Sometimes I got to turn it way up loud."

"I'll sure you'll do the right thing. Now you run along. I think I hear Mr. Big Ears. He sounds hungry."

"Really? You got some good ears, Mister. I didn't hear him."

Roger said, "You better run along and feed him. Nothin' more pitiful than a hungry bunny."

"Okay. Bye." George ran about ten feet and stopped. He turned around. "You guys are nice. Can I come back after breakfast and help?"

"Thank you, George," Bill said. "We need to do this on our own, but you've been a big help. Thanks. Take good care of Mr. Big Ears and enjoy your breakfast."

"Okay. Bye again." George ran off to his house and disappeared inside.

"Spunky kid," Said Bill. I hope his parents can work things out. Seems like the kids can get hurt more than the parents when they can't get along."

Roger sighed, "Ain't that the case. I hope so too. I don't believe we'll find much if it rained hard. Rain's good at destroying evidence."

"It is. Let's see what we can find if anything."

Roger said, "It didn't rain in Canaveral Flats last night."

"Welcome to Florida. One neighborhood gets a flooding monsoon, and a nearby one doesn't even get a sprinkle."

"Yup, this tropical weather sure ain't like up north."

"Wait till you experience a hurricane."

Roger rolled his eyes. "I can hardly wait. Let's see what we can find if anything."

"Okay."

"Hey, you think Mr. Big Ears would make a good name for the donkey?"

"It fits, but no. I think you can do better."

"I think so too. I'll keep searching. Maybe I'll keep him for a while."

They give the area a thorough checking out, but found nothing unusual. The rain had destroyed any footprints the intruders may have left. After this, the men set to digging up the area around the spring, but found nothing of interest though they dug all day. George checked on them regularly from his bedroom window viewpoint. About 4 PM, they decided to call it a day.

"I was hoping we'd find something, at least a little gemstone, anything," Roger said.

"Well, at least we know it's unlikely we'll find anything more here. I don't think the people who've been watching us all day know that."

"I had the feeling we were being watched. That boat that's been sitting way out there trying to pretend they're fishing."

"That's the one."

Roger said, "Let's mess with them. Let's pretend we found something important. You know, drop down on our knees, hoot and holler, and fill that old nylon bag you brought along with something. We did find a chunk of coquina rock."

"That will do. Are you ready?"

"Anytime you are."

"Okay. Go!"

The men gave a performance that would have brought down the house, and were sure the people on the boat took the bait. They left their tools where they lay and ran up to their truck with the heavy stone in the bag and drove off quickly. They stopped on the far side of the church out of view of the boat people. "That was fun," Roger said.

"Yeah, and I think the rats took the bait."

"I know they did. Now we have to be ready for whatever they plan."

"We do. And we need a plan to catch some rats."

Roger said, "What have you have in mind? I hear the wheels

turning."

"Patience, please. Give me a little time to work out the detail. I think I can make it even better. Have I ever led you wrong?"

"Not yet. Don't make this the first time."

"I'll try not to. The first time could be the last time."

"It could. I'd rather not have to improvise on the spot."

"Yeah. What could possibly go wrong?"

# Chapter 30

It was a hot afternoon, much too hot for this time of year. Roger sat in his La-Z-Boy chair in front of a fan that cooled him a little even if all as it blew the sweltering Florida air. Something was better than nothing. K9 lay on the cool concrete floor and panted. The donkey stood under a shade tree and nibbled at some grass. Roger had to shoo the cat away. She wanted to lie on his lap, but he needed that for some papers he was reading on recent developments. The fan was on low. He wished he could have it on high, but when he had put it on high earlier, his papers had been blown away and scattered. Some good and helpful ideas don't always end well.

A truck stopped on the road in front of his trailer. Bill. The donkey looked at Bill with his ears on full alert, but quickly went back to grazing.

Roger watched as Bill got out of the truck and hopped the gate. *Wonder what he wants?* Bill didn't seem to be in any hurry as he advanced toward the trailer.

"Hey, Roger. How's it goin'?"

"Fair to middlin'. As an old redneck fella once told me when asked that question, 'Alright. I ain't been shot at, and I ain't had to shot nobody back,' so life was good."

Bill laughed. "I've had days I felt like that. And I think I know some of the rednecks you could be quoting."

"What's on your little pea-picking mind as Tennessee Ernie Ford would ask?"

"Got any cold beer?"

"You know I do. You want one?"

"I thought you'd never ask."

Roger gave Bill the usual dirty look when he asked the same dumb question. "Get one for me too. Man, it's hot enough to fry an egg on a sidewalk today."

Bill went in the trailer and got two beers. He handed one to Roger, and two pssshh sounds were heard. K9 raised her head, gave them a quick look, and went back to sleep.

Bill said, "This weather ain't normal for this time of year. Just you wait. Cold weather's coming. I can feel it. We're due for a freeze." He took a sip. "How's the donkey doing? He didn't bray like he usually does when I show up."

"I think he's getting used to being here and also to you. He doesn't like the mailman for some reason."

"No one likes the mailman. All they bring are junk mail, bad news, and bills."

"So true, Bill. Any luck with finding him, the donkey that is, not the mailman, a real home?"

"Nope. It's not looking good. I checked with the county again. Their farms are still full of abandoned large animals. They had to put a couple down for lack of space when they came in. I'm afraid that would be donkey's fate too, if you say you can't keep him, and I have to turn him over to the county. Has he been any trouble? Has he bit you or something?"

"No biting. No trouble other than the one time he strayed. Overall, he's very aware of what's going on and brays loudly when he sees something or someone new. He makes a pretty good watchdog 24/7, and I haven't had to see the grass around here gets cut. The donkey's been keeping things trimmed up really good."

"Roger, is he getting along better with K9?"

"'Bout the same. They tolerate each other and keep their distance from each other."

"How's your day been?"

"Crazy. Criminals aren't usually the sharpest tacks in the box. I had to arrest a young woman trying to defraud a merchant. She tried to claim a five hundred dollar prize on an altered lottery card. If she'd checked closer, she would have seen her original number was a five thousand dollar winner. I asked her why she had done this, and she said she always wanted to win something. Well, she won a free trip to the back door of the county jail."

"Sounds like Forest Gump. Stupid is as stupid does."

"Roger, I got a better one than that. You know where the Burger King is on US 1?"

"Yeah, down by the Port St. John Plaza. What about it?"

"Last night after closing while the crew was cleaning up, they were robbed by two guys. I'm not making up the rest. It's real."

"Don't keep me in suspense. What happened?"

"Seemed our two young men from Cocoa had spent all their money partying and smokin' dope. They were flat broke and had a bad case of the munchies, so they decided to kill two birds with one stone. They'd rob a burger joint. They caught one of the employees dumping trash and forced him to let them in at gunpoint. The thieves wanted all the money in the store, which was quickly put in a paper Burger King bag and given to them. Then they wanted two Whoppers each, but the grill had been turned off. They demanded the Whoppers, and you don't argue with men with guns. They waited in the store during the fifteen minutes it took to reheat the grill and cook the burgers.

"During that time, a motorist driving by saw the two guys sitting in the restaurant with guns on the table in front of them. He called the police and said it looked suspicious. Just as they got their food, one county unit and me showed up with sirens blaring and tires squealing. The crooks ran out the side door with the burgers, but left the stolen money on the table. They ran across US 1 almost gettin' hit and tried to hide in some brush on the land next to the FPL power plant.

"A third unit showed up, a K-9 unit. The dog found them fast and lucky for them, the dog tore into the hamburgers and not them. I can still hear the one guy cussin' and growling about how the dog ate their food, and he didn't get a bite. I told them to be glad the only buns the dog bit was the hamburgers and not theirs, but he was still mad."

Roger laughed, "Taking a bite out of crime that's for sure. America's a great country. You're free to be stupid, but some people sure abuse the privilege." He hesitated. "Bill, you didn't come all the way over here to tell me about some dumb criminals. What's up?"

"We lost 'em."

"Who?"

'Those guys watching us in the boat in the river. We lost 'em."

"How, I know you called as soon as we got to the church. What happened?"

"I don't know. Marine Patrol was right out there ASAP, but there was no trace of them. No boat. No people. Nothin'. They vanished like a hole in the water."

"Bill, that tells me something a little frightening."

"It does. We're not dealing with stupid criminals."

"You took the words right out of my mouth. Those guys are pros, and we need to watch our backs. And they think we've got something valuable they want and I'm of the opinion they'll do whatever it takes to get it."

"Roger, be glad you've got a dog and donkey alarm system watching over you."

"I am. I'll take all the help I can get whether it has two or four feet. Bill, you watch yourself too."

"I will. If anyone needs to leave this game, I don't want it to be you or me."

# Chapter 31

Roger shifted in his La-Z-Boy chair as he slept. His sleepy brain told him something had changed, but the grogginess from too much beer made awakening difficult. Without opening his eyes, he felt for the cat, but she wasn't on his lap. He heard a whimpering sound. K9? No, not K9. Donkey? Yes, it was the donkey. Slowly he opened one eye and saw donkey standing just outside his screened-in porch. And someone was next to him dressed in combat fatigues. Roger's body shuddered, and he woke with a start.

"Hello, white man."

"Shaman! What are you doing here? I haven't seen you since you showed up at the dig at Windover. You nearly scared me out of a month's growth. What do you want?"

"I come for you."

"Why?"

"Someone need help."

"Who?"

"You must come," the Shaman paused and said with a voice more of command than a request. "Now. You must come. Life or death. You must come."

"I haven't had breakfast."

"Man probably die if you don't come. Maybe more."

"It's that serious?"

"Yes. You must come now."

Roger grunted. "Okay, you've got my attention. Glad I trust you. Where we goin'?"

"I show you. Bring medicine. Man may die, doctor."

"Doctor? I'm not that kind of doctor."

"Bring medicine. Man may die."

"Okay, I see you're not going to take no for an answer. I've got a first aid kit inside. Give me a minute."

"Hurry. Man may die."

"Okay. Okay. I'll hurry." Roger went inside and found his first aid kit in the bathroom. He used the toilet quickly and met the Shaman at the trailer door.

"Why are you dressed like this? You're wearing combat fatigues and deck shoes. Last time I met you, you were dressed native, headband and breechcloth and little more."

"Come," the Shaman said. "Hurry."

"Okay. I get the picture. It's urgent, but K9 needs fed."

"Canine and cat eat from bag on porch. Donkey stand guard. Hurry."

"Guess you're one step ahead of me."

"Hurry. We take truck."

"Whatever you say, my brown friend."

The Shaman opened the gate for Roger and closed it behind them and got in the truck.

"Where to now?" Roger asked.

"Left."

"Just left?"

"Left."

"This is weird, but if someone needs help…"

"Someone could die. Turn left now."

Roger turned the truck left and began to drive west on washboard Canaveral Flats Boulevard. "Left here," said the Shaman. They came to a four-way stop. "Now right."

The road took them over the interstate highway and to another four-way stop. "Where to now?" asked Roger.

"Go straight. Man needs help."

Roger drove as directed. The road now was only one lane wide and quickly became two paths. As he drove further, vegetation closed in on the truck and in some places it brushed the top and sides. "How much further?"

"We stop soon."

This didn't comfort Roger. They were running out of road as it grew more rutted and primitive. "Stop," the Shaman said.

"Is this the place?"

"No. Look."

"What's a big black fireman's hose doin' layin' across the road out here?" Roger said.

"Not hose. Snake. Good snake. Indigo snake."

"Snake! That's a snake?" Roger watched as the snake pulled itself across the road. Slowly the tail to the enormous reptile disappeared in the weeds and brush.

"He no hurt you. Good snake. Hurry now."

Roger drove faster than he should have on the road that would make cow paths look like a superhighway. He came to a small semi-cleared area where the road ended. It was big enough to turn around, but only barely.

"Stop," the Shaman said. "Get your medicine, doctor. Now we go by boat. Man need help."

The Shaman was out of the truck in a flash and pulled a strange shaped canoe from under some branches. "Come."

Roger got in the boat, and they were off. It had a small motor, but the Shaman used a pole to propel them and occasionally a paddle. After what Roger guessed was about ten minutes, the slough opened up into the St. John River. The Shaman put the motor down into the river and started it. "We must hurry," he said.

The Shaman guided the boat south across the grayish waters for several miles and turned up a small stream whose color was black a pitch. "Where are we now?" Roger asked.

"Death River."

Roger was sorry he had asked. "How much further?"

"We must hurry."

The stream twisted and turned like a snake having a convulsion, and the lush vegetation closed in on both sides and also the top until there was barely room to pass. They traveled on the meandering stream for some time. It felt like night for lack of sunlight. "Hear that?" the Shaman asked.

"Hear what? All I hear are cicadas."

"We must stop." The Shaman got out and pulled the boat up on a small sand bar. "Be still. You must be quiet. I will return."

"Why?"

"Bad man." Before Roger could protest further, the other man disappeared into the thick undergrowth. He was alone. *Bad man. What*

162

*did he mean, bad man, or did he say bad men? Was he referring to me or someone else?* He soon realized he was not alone. Mosquitoes had found him. He opened the first aid kit and got some DEET mosquito repellent out. He pushed the manual pump down and sprayed the bug juice on himself liberally. He used his hand to spread it on his exposed body parts. He waited. And waited. *What was going on? Had he been abandoned?*

As he sat there, he thought he heard a thud sound, and then a man crying out, but he was not sure. It was behind him somewhere, but it was hard to figure where behind was as they had taken so many twists and turns to get where he sat. He heard another sound. This one was much louder — a gunshot and then a deafening silence. An unnatural silence fell on the already surreal place he found himself in. *What was going on?* He waited and wondered about his fate. *Who would ever find his body out here?* No one knew where he was, except the strange little Shaman who may not be coming back. And Roger wasn't sure that would be a good thing considering the gunshot.

He sat, trying to figure how he had ever gotten himself in this predicament and what he should do if anything. Unable to decide, he waited. And waited. Something was coming through the bushes, something making a lot of noise. A big boar hog with a bad attitude? A panther looking for lunch? Maybe even a skunk ape looking for love? This place smelled terrible enough to have a skunk ape. No wonder it was called Death River. Roger was about to bolt when he saw the Shaman coming through the woods, and he was carrying a handgun.

"Come. We must hurry. Man may be dead."

Roger sighed slightly. He felt he had no other viable option but to go with this crazy man. They got back in the boat, and the Shaman started the engine. They were off, but to where? Roger tried to figure out their direction, but the numerous turns in the small stream only had him more confused. They came to a place where clear water from another stream entered Death River. The Shaman pointed the boat up this new body of crystal clear water. This stream was almost straight compared to the other, and daylight was able to penetrate the tall trees. They traveled for about another five minutes, and the Shaman beached the boat on a sand bar sticking out from the back.

"You here."

Roger wondered where in the world here was. He felt like he had entered a world from one of Captain Kirk's wildest dreams. If he hadn't known better, he would have thought he had left the planet. Sweat ran down Roger's shirt.

"You come. We see man."

Roger followed the Shaman through some brush and onto a trail. Roger wondered what kind of animal had created this, but he wasn't sure he wanted to know. They walked for what seemed a mile at least, and Roger saw a hut, a chickee, made out of palm branches and tree branches.

"Man here. You make better, doctor."

Roger was curious about what he would find, but also fearful. Was the man already dead? For how long? Would the Shaman blame him? He moved some mosquito netting that served as a door to the side and walked in. A large man with shaggy white hair dressed in ragged clothes lay on his side with his back to Roger. He watched his sides rise and fall. *At least he's breathing.*

"Man sick. Help him, doctor."

Roger got closer for a better look. The man looked familiar. Yes, he knew him. It was Del. He had been with the Shaman when they had surprised him at the archaeological dig some time ago. Roger touched his head. He was burning up. "How longs he been like this?"

"Two days. Today worst. My herbs do nothing, so I get you. Help him."

Roger looked the man's entire body over carefully. He saw a small spot on his leg that looked possibly infected. "Do you have any ice here?" Roger felt like a fool asking this, considering where he was. The Shaman seemed to be thinking or maybe puzzled. "Ice," Roger repeated sternly. "Do you have any ice? He needs to be cooled down."

"Lone Cabbage Fish Camp have ice."

"How long would it take to get there and back?"

"Two, maybe three hours. Maybe longer."

Roger shook his head. "That's too long. He could be dead by then. We need to cool him down now and get some medicine in him."

"Stream cool. We put him in stream."

"No way. That shallow water must be 90 degrees. That'll never work."

"Come. I show you."

Roger followed the Shaman for fifty feet through the jungle, and they came to a bubbling spring. The pool it created was about the size of a bathtub.

"Water cool."

Roger put his hand in the liquid, and sure enough, like the man had said, it was cool. This spring had to come from thousands of feet below the ground straight from the Florida Aquifer running below most of the state. Now he knew why he had seen the clear water on the way here.

Roger and the Shaman managed to get Del to his feet one on each side holding him up and walked the staggering man to the spring and sat him down next to it. Roger got his first aid kit and took two Tylenol from it. "Del," Roger said. "Shaman came to my house and got me. I'm trying to help you. You're burning up."

Del's breathing was shallow and rapid. He looked at Roger through one barely open eye. "I know you. You're that professor fellow."

"The Shaman thinks I'm a medical doctor, but I'm a Ph.D. doctor. I think you need to be in a hospital."

Del shook his head. "No physicians. No hospitals. If I die, it won't be there. I won't go."

Roger could see there was no point arguing with him and he wasn't sure Del would make it to the closest hospital alive. "Del, I'll do what we can for you. You need to take these two capsules. They should lower your fever. You've got a little wound on your leg that may be infected. I' m gonna treat it too."

"Okay. You do that, please."

"I'll do what I can to keep you alive."

A sheepish smile came to Del's face. "Yeah, I'm not ready to die. I don't want no preacher to have to lie at my funeral."

Roger laughed. The first capsule went down easy, but Del choked up on the second one. It went down on the second attempt. Roger put some Neosporin on the wound and rubbed some charcoal in it to draw any poison. "That's the best I can do." He turned to the man who had brought him here. "Shaman, now we need to get him in the spring."

As gently as they could, they lowered the feverish man into the cool water. Over the next two days, the sick man slowly grew better. Roger continued the same treatment, and it was working. He kept a close eye on Del's condition. The Shaman came and went mainly bringing in fresh meat and fish, which he cooked over an open fire. Roger noticed the fish seemed to be blind, and he wondered why that was. Blind or not the fish and meat tasted good, especially when it was all there was to eat, and you were hungry.

By the third day, Del was on his feet and walking slowly, but he was weak. After the evening meal, the men sat in a hodgepodge of cast-off chairs the Shaman and Del had salvaged from the St. John River. Roger and Del made small talk, but the third man said little.

The Shaman looked toward them. "I save your life," and then his eyes seemed to gaze away at something distant.

Roger said to Del, "He did save your life. He knew you needed help and came and got me."

"True, he did, but I think he was talking to you, Roger."

"What do you mean?"

"While you were sleeping, I talked with him. He told me how he went for help when his medicine didn't work on me. Some men had staked out your house and were trying to find a way around the big mouth donkey to get to you. Shaman got you out of there in the nick of time. They followed you and him through Canaveral Flats, over the St. Johns, and through the jungle. He took them out at Death River."

Roger looked shocked. "He left me in that place. I thought I had been abandoned, but he was saving me. I heard a man scream and a gunshot. So that's what happened."

"Those bodies are gone forever. You noticed the blind fish?"

"I was curious about that."

"Part of Death River is open to the aquifer. No one knows how deep it is. The Shaman knows where the holes are better than I do. The fish we pull up from the depths are all blind. I've dropped over three hundred feet of line down and still not hit bottom. You can bet he dropped the men who wanted to get their hands on you in one of those holes. Not only am I a lucky man to be alive, but so are you."

"Del, do you think I should thank him? I'd like to."

"It won't be necessary. He said he was thankful you came with him and pulled me back from out of the jaws of death. Any debt you owned, you paid back by saving me, his friend. It's all even, and everyone is alive and happy. Any idea who those guys he took out were?"

"I do, but I can't be 100% sure. I only hope whoever it was, thinks twice about trying it again."

"For your sake, I do too. What're you gonna do when you leave here? How are you gonna explain your absence and vanishing?"

"I may just say the Shaman needed me. Think that will work?"

"Roger, I think Chief of Police Bill Kenney would understand."

"I do too, but I'm not so sure about some others."

"It'll work out. Trust me."

# Chapter 32

The black four-door Chevy Impala slowly traveled up Indian River Drive and stopped at the only house on the east side of the road. A woman dressed in a black bodysuit walked toward the vehicle from the house. The headlights pierced the darkness and reflected off her tight clothing. She opened the door and got it. "How did it go?" the driver asked. The car pulled back onto the narrow road.

"It went well," she said. "I walked out. You didn't hear any gunshots, and I didn't have to blow up the house."

"I see," he said. "Our equipment suppresses the sound of gunshots, so no one else got a shot off. That's good. Is the house going to blow up soon?"

"No," she said. "It wasn't necessary. It would be a shame to destroy such a pleasant looking building, though I doubt ODESSA will continue using it much longer after what's happened tonight."

They drove another half mile through the early morning darkness. Bright light from a thunderous explosion turned the area where the house on the east side of the river stood into daylight. Fire ravished the remains of the structure as a tremendous roar passed over them. "I thought you said the house wasn't going to blow up? Your little joke made a strong statement."

"Husband, that wasn't my work. I took out the old man and made my exit. That wasn't my doing. Let's get out of here."

He sped up and went faster than was safe on the narrow, twisty road lined with trees of all kinds, oaks and sable palms mainly. Many a naive young man full of alcohol and testosterone had crashed into one of these and then burned while tempting fate on this challenging road, but the man handled the road like a racecar driver on the winding track of the Monaco Grand Prix. Many hours of hard training and a few crashes had given him the skills he used tonight. And the old sedan wasn't what it seemed. Some modification had made the 4000-pound beast as agile as a speeding cheetah.

He pulled onto US 1 and drove north just a hair over the speed limit. A fire truck and a police car whizzed by him going south. Both people in the vehicle noted their passing, but said nothing. He zigzagged through the maze of streets in Port St. John, often circling around. He had to make sure they weren't being followed. They weren't. She said, "Looks like no one's following us. Who do you think's responsible for blowing up the house?"

"I have my suspicions. We're not the only ones that had an ax to grind with his type. The Americans have a handful of agencies, official or black ops. It could be the Brits, the Israelis, or someone else. Maybe even the French. I'm just glad they waited till you were gone. I don't want to lose you. I nearly have several times. We've been through a lot together."

"Yes," she said. "I think it was the Israelis. They usually try not to destroy innocent life, even that of a for-hire prostitute. It could have been a time bomb, and we just were lucky."

He said, "You can plan all you want, but a little luck can come in handy." His gloved hand touched her gloved hand, and she pulled it back.

"Don't touch me. I feel so filthy after what I've just done."

"That's good. I know the feeling."

She said, "What was it like for you, you know with the old homosexual German?"

"It wasn't something I enjoyed. You have to use the right bait. It was a job we had to do. In some ways, it was probably easier for me than you. We knew he was impotent, so when I told him I had a little blue pill to fix that, he jumped at the idea and took it willingly. I merely talked to him as the drug took effect. It's amazing what people are willing to believe when they want to. Reminds me of politicians –

tell the gullible what they want to hear. It doesn't matter if it's real or not. It's often bad for them, but who cares?

"After a little numbness, his muscles became totally unresponsive. Then I showed him the pictures of some of his victims and smothered him with a pillow, a far easier death than he deserved. It was so easy, but I hate to think of the day when I take a life, even those that deserve to die for their crimes, with as much thought as when I swat a fly."

"Me too, husband."

"So how did it go for you?"

She said, "He questioned why the usual girl he called for wasn't there. He seemed satisfied with my explanation of her being moved on the circuit to New York City. I did know about the drink he liked. He said to pour two, and I did. I managed to get the drug in the drinks without his notice, but the cautious man took mine, but it had the drug too only I'd taken a counter-dose to offset the effects. He ran his hand down my hip and began removing my clothes, but then the drug started to kick in quickly. The new catalyst worked fine, better than fine.

"He realized what was happening, but it was too late by then. I had to keep him from falling. I put him on the bed face up and showed him pictures of his family. I told him we'd killed them all. It was paybacks for his war crimes. You should've seen his eyes. And then I took his hand and touched it to my breast. I asked him if it was good. You should have seen the hatred in those eyes. And then I smothered him while groaning like we were having sex. The information we had on him said he liked groaners. I did it mainly in case the guard was listening. When I came out, I shut the door behind me. The guard wasn't far away. I told him his boss had said it was his birthday, and I gave him a special treat, and now the boss was sleeping. The guard said tomorrow was his birthday, and I told him to call tomorrow. He liked that much more than I did."

Mr. Smith said, "And now he's gone too."

170

"I loved the idea of how the old man died thinking we took his whole family away from him, husband. I know we don't operate like that though others do. Only he's responsible for what he did during the Great War."

"True. May we never get that ruthless or callous."

"I heartily agree. People like that aren't human."

"Mrs. Smith, that's why they need killing no matter how long it takes to track them down."

"Nazis aren't the only ones."

"I wish they were the only ones, but the communists have given us so many more – Stalin's henchmen, Mao's killers, and Pol Pot's butchers in Cambodia to name a few."

"Don't forget the genocides in Africa."

Mrs. Smith said, "I wish I could. I guess there'll always be a demand for our kind of talent."

"People and governments will always be willing to pay to see those who escaped justice are brought to justice one way or the other," he said.

"When they can't do it, they come to our organization. We have rules too, but the organization wants results and's willing to look the other way if it's necessary to get the job done."

"Very true. I told my Nazi John the treasure theft he'd masterminded would never reach its destination. He reacted strongly even though drugged. That hit him where it hurt. Too bad the stolen treasure will never be recovered."

"Why not, husband? What haven't you told me?"

"One of our operatives sent the yacht and all on it to Davy Jones locker. They sank it in one of the deepest places in the Atlantic Ocean."

"Probably just as well," she said. "It won't cause any more trouble there. But maybe Neptune will find it and give it to his wife and twelve daughters, and they'll fight over it."

"Could be. You never know. I heard Tim Mace made it back to his professor job up north. I'm glad he knew Roger from the past and was able to help when he was needed."

"Yes. It was a stroke of luck. Sometimes, you have to make your own luck. This much I know for sure, Mr. Smith. I believe we need to shower together, and you wash the grim off my body. Are you up for that, Mr. Smith? Are you feeling lucky?"

"Well," he said. "A good, thorough, and sensuous scrubbing will definitely make me rise to the occasion."

She smiled knowingly. "That's good, my husband. I love you. Don't change." She scooted close to him and kissed his cheek.

"I love you too. After a hard day of work, it makes you happy to go home."

"Very true. Step on the gas. I need a bath ASAP or sooner."

A grin came to his face. "Anything for you, love. We got the job done. Let's see if we can enjoy our down time. You never know when duty will call again."

"True, and it could be very soon if I read the signs right."

He nodded, said nothing more, and drove on into the night.

# Chapter 33

Roger walked through the door to the office of the Riverside Baptist Church. He saw Pastor Nassey sitting behind the secretary's desk doing paperwork. A woman Roger guessed at being between 50 and 55 sat in an overstuffed chair nearby and was dressed like a professional woman. The pastor looked up from his work. "Well, hello, Roger. You're early." He rose and extended his hand.

"Good to see you again, Pastor," he said as he shook his hand. Roger looked at the woman who had risen from the chair.

"Roger, this is Eva Egged. She's a friend of mine."

"Not **the** Eva Egged? Bill Kenney mentioned that name to me recently. He said she lived locally and was a survivor of a Nazi prison camp. Is that you?"

"Yes. I'm one and the same. I've known the good pastor for years, and I know who Bill Kenney is, Chief of Police for Canaveral Flats. Though the pastor and I have our differences and disagreements, we've managed to remain friends, good friends I might add, for a long time."

Her voice seemed to have traces of a German or even a Yiddish accent in it, maybe both. Roger tried to place it, but couldn't.

"And I want it to remain that way, Eva," The pastor said. "Roger, I took the liberty of asking her to come and sit in with us tonight while we talked. Is that okay with you?"

Before he could answer, she said, "Mr. Pyles. You won't hurt my feeling if you say no. I'm always willing to help, and the pastor asked as a personal favor."

"Roger, I invited her because I thought she could help."

"Pastor, the first time I met you, I knew you were an honorable man. If she's got your seal of approval, she's fine with me." He extended his hand to her, which she shook. "Pleased to meet you, Miss or is it Mrs. Egged?"

"You can call me Eva. That would be fine with me. And thank you for trusting me to sit in on your meeting with the pastor."

"Well, Eva it is then. I've got some questions for you too, if you don't mind."

"I'll help where I can."

"Okay, now we all know each other, let's go into my office and get started."

Roger said, "Sure thing Pastor," and he headed in followed by Eva with the pastor at the end of the pack. They each found a comfortable chair and took a seat.

The pastor said, "Eva, would you like to start with a prayer?"

"My Jewish book of prayers hasn't been used much lately, but I have one. Here goes, 'Y'-va-re-ch'-cha A-do-nai v'-yish-m'-re-cha; ya-er Adonai pa-nev a-le-cha vi-chu-ne-ka; yi-sa A-do-nai pa-nav a-le-cha.v'ya-sem-l'-cha shalom.'"

"I think I've heard that before. It does sound vaguely familiar," Roger said.

"May the Lord bless you and keep you. May His eyes shine down upon you and be gracious unto you. May the Lord place His countenance upon you and give you peace always. Amen," Pastor Nassey said. "That Roger, was the Priestly Blessing from the book of Numbers, chapter 6 verses 24, 25, and 26."

"I think Rabbi Katz of the Merritt Island Synagogue prayed that prayer while I was with him. You guys know him?"

The pastor looked at Eva and smiled. "We do. He's a great guy, right, Eva?"

"He is, a little too religious and orthodox for my tastes, but as the pastor said, a great guy, in spite of those two flaws."

Her words brought smiles to both men's faces.

"Roger, what was it you wanted to see me about when you asked for this meeting?"

"Well, Pastor, you know I've been through some tough times. I got railroaded out of my position at the college I taught at for the crimes of questioning the current status quo and thinking. My wife and son died in a car wreck about two years ago. I've had attempts on my life recently and did I say I drink to excess daily? If I didn't, I drink too much and sometimes repeat myself. Other than that, my world is all butterflies and a bed of roses."

Eva said, "You're sarcastic and down on yourself also."

Roger sighed, "Yeah, that too, but who's counting? Guess you could say, my life's a mess and doesn't seem to be getting any better."

"Roger," the pastor said. "I think you have a lot going for you even if it seems like you're in a deep pit where the sun barely shines. Your coming here tonight tells me you're seeking help. That's good. And you're willing to talk about your problems. You know you have them. Ever tried to help someone who wouldn't talk about their problems or admit to even having them?"

"Yeah. Me. I know what that's like. A friend of mine by the name of Tim visited lately. He left right before you showed up at my trailer when the donkey problem arose."

"Oh, yes. How could I forget that?"

"Anyway Pastor, Tim told me a story about a donkey at the bottom of a deep well. The farmer saw no way to get the animal out. He saw the creature as not worth saving. Too much effort would be required, so he decided to bury the donkey in the dry well. He shoveled dirt in on the donkey who brayed wildly as he realized what was happening. He got quiet, and the farmer thought he had seen the last of the donkey. To the farmer's amazement, the donkey was climbing on top of the dirt he dumped in, and the donkey crawled out covered in dirt but alive when the hole was nearly filled up. Pastor, I feel like I've been dumped on. I want to be like that dumb beast. I want to climb out of the darkness, the hole I've been living in. What do I do?"

The two other people in the room were silent for a while. Roger could tell they were thinking, and he had no desire to rush them. The pastor was the first to speak. "Guess that old donkey wasn't so dumb after all. What was meant to bury him was his salvation. He quit crying about the problem and figured a way out. Roger, you're seeking a way out. Talking about your difficulties, the trauma you've experienced is a step to your healing."

"Grief and suffering seem to be universal in the human race," Roger said. "I know Eva is all too familiar with those, but what do you know about those personally, Pastor? I know you've seen your share of man's inhumanity to man in your work."

"I have. On a personal level, I lost a daughter much too soon. She had a heart condition we didn't know about. She collapsed on the floor at her apartment and died alone. My wife was grief-stricken and now deals with depression. And I've got two other wayward children

175

messing in things they shouldn't, and I've been known to drink too much in days gone by. Sound familiar? I'll leave it at that for now."

"I see. Pastor, the more I learn about people I'm coming to realize a smiling face can hide a lot of hurt inside."

"It is. Roger, there were days I used my smiley face to mask the pain inside. I guess we're all like that in some ways. We want people to think we've got it all together when we don't."

"Very true."

"Have you considered going to Alcoholics Anonymous?"

"Pastor, it's an option I haven't ruled out, but not right now."

Eva spoke, "Roger, have you grieved for your losses?"

"I have, and sometimes it gets so dark, I want to crawl into a hole and die. I wish it had been me that died and not my family."

She said, "Everyone grieves differently. One of the greatest dangers is isolating ourselves from others and not letting them know how it's affecting us. So many of my family died in the Holocaust. For years, I kept my feelings inside. You had to just to survive in the Nazi prison camps. I did that for years afterward until one day I totally fell apart. It was a long road to recovery. Fortunately, I had friends who were there to help. They didn't always understand, and even when they tried to help would say the wrong thing, and it would hurt, but they were always there for me. That got me through the unbearable hard times."

"Eva, I'm still having a problem with suffering in this world. I've talked some with Pastor Nassey on this matter. What you've seen and experienced is far worse than anything the pastor or I know. How can an all-powerful God allow such things to happen?"

She put her hand to her mouth and seemed to be thinking. "That question has been asked since mankind first wrote his thoughts down. The pastor and I have a little different take on this, but for the most part, we agree. Sometimes I wonder if God didn't just create the world and put it on autopilot, but other times I look at my scriptures and see the prophesies where Israel will become a nation again, and know only someone outside of time who cares could do that. It's the only book like that anywhere.

"Roger, there's a lot of dirty people in this world, but there's soap available to change that. Just because people don't or won't bathe is not a reason to blame the Creator."

The Pastor said, "Roger, she's right about how we see this question somewhat different. I believe this universe and the order within it is all too big and complex to have happened by mere chance. I'd say it's impossible. That being said, are we only an insignificant speck on a glob of dirt in an obscure corner of the universe? I don't believe so. I believe He put in everyone the desire to know Him. It's why man is the only creature who asks such questions. Some people mock or deny this, but the hunger for God is still there and can only be satisfied by getting to know our Creator in a personal way. Why is there suffering? I'd call it sin. Eva prefers to call it evil. Either way, it's like a deadly cancer affecting our entire lives and everyone in this world. Roger, I don't know how much of this advice, you'll take or are ready to take, but this I know for sure – keep moving. Life is one day at a time. Just because you experienced failure one day, doesn't mean you're a failure. It means you're human. Failure is not getting up and trying again."

Eva spoke, "Very true. Roger, all people have choices. My concept of God is a little different from the pastor's, but I believe He gave us the freedom to choose, to determine our actions. Without this ability, we'd be little more than robots only able to do what was programmed into us. The Nazi's choices in my homeland of Germany resulted in the deaths of millions of human beings. People don't always use their freedoms wisely. Freedom is not about being born into a perfect world. Freedom is about being born into a world where you have the power to change things, including ourselves."

"Is that what keeps you going?"

Pastor Nassey and Eva nodded. He said, "There are days when it seems like we can't or aren't making any difference. Let me tell you a story. After a storm on the Delaware beaches, millions of starfish have washed ashore. One man could be seen picking up starfish and throwing them into the sea. A second man came and laughed at his efforts. What difference would his puny actions make when the need was so great, he asked. The first man continued what he was doing and said each time he threw one back, 'Made a difference to him.' Roger,

177

we can do only what we can do to change ourselves and the world. Do what you can and pray there are others who will help. You may be the one who will help.

"This line of work brings you in contact with a lot of people with problems. I remember being on a stakeout for some break-ins we believed were drug-related. As it turned out, we guessed right and arrested two people, known drug offenders, a guy and his girlfriend and companion in crime. The guy told me he was tired of how his life was going and wanted to change. I've heard that a lot from people when they're arrested. He asked if he could write to me, and we exchanged letters over his four-year incarceration. He's been out for several years now and walking the straight and narrow roadway and working at trying to save junkies from themselves at a shelter. His girlfriend got out and went back to drugs. She overdosed shortly after her release." Phil Nassey sighed. "Two different people. Two different choices. One chooses wisely. One didn't, and their choices were the difference between life and death.

"Roger, I expect the name Viktor Frankl is familiar to you," Eva said.

"It is. I read his book a long time ago."

"Good, in *Man's Search for Meaning*, he tells of two brothers in the same Nazi concentration camp. Same heredity, same environment. One behaved like a saint. The other like a pig."

"That's a pretty low description for a Jew to call another Jew."

"It is. Frankl pointed out how all have the power to choose how they will react to their circumstances. We were given the power of choice. Some people don't want to take responsibility for their actions. They blame everything but themselves. It's society's fault, the environment, the schools, their circumstances. Society is made up of individuals, and for there to be social justice, people must take the blame for how things are. Accept responsibility and do something about it. I all too well realize people find themselves dealing with conditions created by someone else's bad choices or mishaps. This world is far from perfect, and if it was perfect like in the beginning, we would make bad choices, sin, just like Adam did."

Roger was silent for a moment. "You guys both know about what happened next door. Do you really believe that after that tragedy? How do you explain evil like that?"

Eva said, "I do. Doing evil is a choice, and it harms not only the one who does it but others whether next door or in the concentration camps."

Pastor Nassey said. "What happened next door was unspeakable evil at its worst. Little George's father did horrible things. He blamed his problems on his family, especially his wife, and he wanted to cause as much pain as possible. Shooting George, his grandma, and then himself to death solved nothing. Wounding his wife when he shot her is only the least of her pain now. If I didn't believe there was good and evil, there would be no difference between Mother Teresa and Adolph Hitler. I went over to help when I heard what was going on. They let me in being I'm an auxiliary officer and a chaplain. I tried to comfort George's mother best I could. I believe George and his grandma are in a better place, Heaven. Grandma was a believer who attended this church.

"I saw how people deal with death. One deputy was a young woman with a child about George's age. She did the best she could to do her duties, but finally retreated from the house and asked for a replacement. She couldn't understand how a parent could do that. Some of the other deputies used dark humor to deal with the horrible scene. I know we're more than just flesh and blood. We have a soul that exists eternal. A body may die, but the soul continues to exist."

Roger looked at Eva, "Do you believe this?"

"Though we look at things differently, I've come to basically the same conclusion. Our existence is more than physical, and there will be a day of accounting before our Creator. I believe He loves us enough to give us the ability to love, reason, and interact with others. Some people use this freedom to do terrible things. We call this evil. That's what I believe."

No one said anything for a few moments. Roger could visualize six year old George, little Curious George. A glimmer of a smile came to him as he thought of their encounter, but George's cherub face changed into that of his son, the one he'd just learned of recently. The smile left his face and one of concern took its place.

Roger spoke, "I think my mental plate is full and overflowing. I'd like some time to digest all this."

"It's taken me a long time to get to this point of understanding," the pastor said. "I wouldn't expect anything else from another."

Eva spoke, "Pastor Nassey took the words right out of my mouth. Our understanding comes one bite at a time." She stopped. "I think we've said all there is to say for now, but I'd more than welcome an opportunity to talk with you alone or together again in the future."

Roger and the pastor agreed, and the meeting broke up after a little chit-chat and some salutations.

Hours later, Roger lay kicked back in his La-Z-Boy chair at his trailer. Darkness had come several hours ago. K9 slept on the floor nearby, and a tortie cat was on Roger's lap. He stroked her fur as he thought about what he had discussed with the pastor and Eva. He nodded off, and when he awoke was not sure what time it was. A quick look at his watch told him it was a little after midnight. He knew he wouldn't be able to solve all the problems in the world, but maybe he was closer to solving some of his. The world was a funny place. The Babylonians thought it was flat. Roger stroked the cat's fur slowly. *Those Babylonians should have known better. Cats would have pushed everything over the sides.*

Tomorrow was another day. Each day had enough troubles of its own. He would deal with tomorrow's problems when they came. The cat still on Roger's lap stretched and looked at him. Her eyes seemed to say, "What are you doing up at this hour? Rest. You'll need it for tomorrow." She closed her eyes and went back to sleep. Roger smiled as he ran his hand over her furry head and drifted off to sleep. Tomorrow would take care of itself.

# Chapter 34

January 27, 1986

Roger pulled the blanket tighter. If it got any colder, he'd be sleeping in his trailer rather than outside in the La-Z-Boy on the screened-in porch. He heard K9 growling and opened his eyes. Chief of Police Bill Kenney was walking down the dirt road to his trailer.

"Easy K9. Don't bite him. He'll leave a bad taste in your mouth even licking your butt won't get rid of," Roger said softly.

"What's that you say?" Bill shouted.

"I told him you were friendly, and it was okay."

Bill walked closer. "That's good to know. I can't say I always get a good reception like that." K9 laid back down. Bill entered the screened-in room and took a seat. "It's getting colder. I had to wear a jacket this morning."

"I didn't think Florida got cold."

"We usually get a light frost or two around here yearly. Tomorrow's supposed to be colder. I don't know if it will affect the shuttle launch or not."

"Really? You mean to tell me with all the millions NASA gets they didn't consider weather conditions?"

Bill said, "I guess they could postpone launching Challenger till it warms up. We'll see. Gonna be a good launch if it goes. Got that teacher on board and an Israeli as part of the crew."

"I'll make a point of watching. Think I can see it from here?"

"I know you can, but you'd see it better at the river."

"I thought that might be the case. Are you working tomorrow, Bill? Last launch we were watching it from your boat on the Indian River."

"I'll be goin' right down US 1 like Neal Armstrong."

"Bill, you lost me on that one."

"When the astronauts Apollo 11 blasted off from the Moon, Neal Armstrong said that. I hope my ride's as smooth and trouble-free. Rog, you live here very long, and you'll pick up a lot of space knowledge and trivia."

"Cool."

"Old buddy, you wouldn't believe it, but some people want to park on the four-lane when they can't find a place to pull off."

"Yeah, I would. You can always bet on stupid."

"I'm afraid so. Honestly Roger, most of the people I have to deal with are pretty good and no real trouble. That's not to say there aren't some evil ones you have to ID and deal with. Now, the stupid ones are some of the funniest but most likely to get themselves or you hurt. They're the reason we have to put directions and warnings on bottles of shampoo."

Roger said, "Ain't that the truth. So what's new in the world today? I haven't read my newspapers for a week or more."

"I knew that, Mr. Obvious. That stack of newspapers kinda gave it away. Where should I start? Hmm. A yacht that left Port Canaveral some time ago has been reported missing. The Coast Guard is looking for it but hasn't found any trace of it. The Fire Marshall's report on the house along the river that blew up is in. They said it was a gas explosion."

"That area got gas?"

"None piped to the house underground. They said it was bottled gas that exploded, though I don't ever remember seeing a tank outside when I've driven by. Guess it could have been inside."

"You think so?"

"No. It's odd and suspicious, but until I have something more to go on, I'll accept the story, but keep my doubts to myself. By the way, Roger, the two bodies found have not been identified. As you can imagine, they were burned up and in bad shape. The house was titled to a company out of New York City. Turns out it was nothing more than a shell for some group out of South America, and I'd bet a dollar to a donut, that's a shell too. It will be difficult to find out who's behind all this, if ever."

"Yeah, that's very curious. Suspicious explosions. Dead bodies everywhere without answers as to who make them that way or why. And nothing new on the stolen museum treasure. Seems we've a lot of unanswered questions."

"Yup," Bill said. Somebody somewhere knows something. Things have a way of eventually being revealed."

"Gonna have to agree with you on that one," Roger said. "In the meantime, I'll keep plodding along."

"Roger, I've seen cases solved simply because the investigators never quit."

"Yup. Any new interesting stories on your cop work to tell me?"

"No. With this upcoming launch, I've been busy with traffic control, and that's usually pretty mundane. I had to write a few tickets to people who deserved it. Good grief, if they'd only be polite and cooperate, I usually let them off with a warning if the offense isn't too great."

"Bill, you get a lot of crying women?"

"I've had my share over the years. I hate to give a crying woman with a sob story a ticket. Don't tell anyone, but they usually get off scot-free."

"You can trust me. I won't. Hey, I heard the Riverside Baptist Church is getting a new roof. It seems some broker put an option on one of the jewels dug up at the church. The church gets the money now, and they can use it however they see fit. And the broker gets the first option on purchase of the jewels."

"That's good to know. So what's new with you, Roger?"

"Lester came around, and I paid him for the electrical work he did on my trailer. He gave me some advice on some financial matters and I moved some money to a place where it can grow faster. The donkey's starting to think this is his new home, and I got a call from the governor's office. They said they still are interested in me heading up the archaeological dig at Windover."

Bill said, "I hear a but coming."

Roger nodded, "But funding had to be moved around, and some committees are continuing to drag their feet."

"That sounds familiar. The people who've been running things for decades keep telling us government's the problem. Just reelect them, and they'll fix it."

"That's my take on it too, Bill. I ain't holding my breath."

"So what are you thinking of doing?"

"Well, all the cases I've been working on seem to have reached a conclusion or dead end. I thought about going home up North for a while. I'd like to see some old friends and visit my son and wife's graves."

"I can see why you'd want to get away for a while."

"My cousin Suzy's not doing too good. She was that one special cousin everyone has. Did I ever tell you about her?"

"I can't say you did."

"When I was a mean little kid, she came to live with us. Her parents were having some troubles, and my parents took her till things got settled. A month stay turned into a year. I had to share my room with her. I tormented her a lot, even though I grew to like her as a friend. I remember one time a neighbor kid got some fireworks around the Fourth of July. We had an old outhouse, and instead of going to the bathroom inside when we played outside, we'd use it. Suzy was in there one afternoon, and we got the great idea of throwing some firecrackers through the crack at the bottom. This was back in the days when little girls all wore dresses. She came flying out of there with her panties down around her ankles. She saw us laughing our heads off, figured out what happened, and came after us with blood in her eye. The other kid ran for home, and she caught me and gave me the thrashing I had coming. I never did that again.

"Fortunately, she wasn't one to hold a grudge and forgave me. Over the years, we tried to keep in touch. She was a sympathetic ear when my life was falling apart."

"This isn't exactly the best time to go up North. It's January, you know."

"Bill, I remember the Januarys in the northland all too well. If I do go, I'll take a plane from Orlando to Baltimore or Pittsburgh. I'll see where I can get the best flight fares and rent-a-car deals. The distance to the old home place is about the same either way."

"A road trip around Florida would be a lot warmer and convenient. You get tired of traveling; you can turn around and come home."

"True, lots of things to do and see in the Sunshine State – museums, beaches, St. Augustine, Miami, Mickey Mouse. Maybe even head on down to the Keys. Take the Overseas Highway all the way to Key West."

"Sounds like fun, but you could have a lot of fun, but get in a lot of trouble down in the Keys. A guy I know named Jesse McDermitt seems to be having all kinds of adventures down there."

"I'll keep that in mind," Roger said, "but who'd take care of my critters? This place is starting to look like a zoo."

"I'm sure Lester would do it if you asked. I might even if you asked nicely."

Roger gave Bill a dirty look and growled, "I always ask nicely." He paused. "Hey, you didn't help yourself to a beer. What's up? Lester been fussin' at you about doing that on the job?"

"A little, but today, it's kinda cool. I don't want a cold beer. Got any coffee or hot cocoa?"

"No cocoa, not even instant and you'd have to brew a new pot."

"Never mind," Bill said. "Anything else new with you?"

"I've been thinking about what I want to do in the future."

"So you've decided on beauty school?"

"Naw. I don't think I have the personality for it. Someone would complain, and I'd probably bite their heads."

"True."

"Hey, you didn't have to agree so fast."

"Roger, I don't think beauty school is the place for you."

"Me neither, but it was a humorous thought. Maybe, I'll become a writer."

"Really?"

"I'm good at telling stories. It used to get me in trouble growing up."

Bill said, "I can see that. I'm sure you could tell some whoppers."

Roger gave his friend a hairy eyeball. "Thanks for the vote of confidence, old buddy."

"Anytime," Bill chucked. "But what makes you think you can be a writer?"

"Well, I've written some short stories and just the other day while I was waiting in line at the drive-thru at the burger place, my imagination started to run wild. I saw four palm trees together that seemed to shape a W. Remember the old movie where a bunch of people find a guy who just was in a terrible wreck, and he tells them about a huge cache of money hidden near a big W?"

"The Great Race?"

"Close, but no cigar. It was *It's a Mad, Mad, Mad, Mad World*."

"Yeah, that's the one. Had a whole bunch of big-name actors in it and a lot of other famous people who did cameos."

"Yup, Bill, you're right."

"And you think you could write one that good?"

"I'll never know until I try."

"Why not, Roger? Go for it."

"Bill, as I was sitting in line, my mind was moving a mile a minute. I thought about the gal in the drive-thru window. What if she saw a gun on the seat of the black sedan in front of me? What if he gave her an envelope full of money with a note with cryptic directions, maybe even veiled threats as to what could happen if she didn't follow them? Or how would she react if a flying saucer got in line and the green aliens on board wanted a Number 3 Animal style?"

"Roger, it might work. That imagination of yours sure helps with police investigations. Why not try your hand at writing? I remember an episode of Leave it to Beaver."

"I remember that show. What's it got to do with writing?"

Bill said, "This is the best I can remember it. In one episode, Beaver wants to become a writer and Mom, June Cleaver, asks why. He says because it's neat to make things up and get paid for it. His brother Wally says publishing company guys fix your grammar and spelling and commas and junk like that. Some of them even holler the whole book into a recording machine. Of course, the Beav wants one of those machines. Daddy Ward advises him to start a journal. Somerset Maugham did. Wally says a guy with a name like that should be a linebacker for the Steelers, but Dad assures him the man was a writer. He tells Beav when he gets an idea, write it down. You never know when it will develop into a good story."

"And they all live happily ever after."

"They always did on those 60's TV shows."

"I don't think it's that easy. You know, I bet lots of people have stories in them they'll never write."

"Roger, I think multitudes go to the grave with the music still in them. If you have a story in you, let it out."

"Thanks for the vote of confidence. I guess if it doesn't work out, there's always beauty school."

Bill rolled his eyes. "I'm leaving. It's getting deep around here, and I don't have a shovel. Let me know what your plans are before you take a trip or act on any rash ideas."

"You know me."

"That's why I said that."

"Bill, I wouldn't do anything you wouldn't."

"That's what I'm afraid of. Roger, let me know what you decide. I'll be in touch if anything new develops on the cases we've been working on. Gotta go. See yah."

"Yeah, see ya."

Roger watched as Bill walked to his truck. He made a U-turn and headed in the direction of US 1. Traffic was probably bad on the highway with the launch scheduled for tomorrow. He thought he'd go down to the Indian River and watch. He'd park at Riverside Baptist Church. The Youth Group was doing a fundraiser and charging people to park on the property, and he bet the church would have their bathrooms available for anyone, possibly him, who might need the facilities.

He kicked his feet out in front of him, put his hands behind his head, and stretched. A groan passed through his lips. K9 jumped to her feet with her ears erect and gave a questioning bark. "I'm okay girl. Just stretching and thinking. Places to go. Things to do. Law and order to keep."

He wondered about the Queen's Jewels and the treasure in the 1715 Fleet. Somehow, he didn't think the last chapter or chapters in the book about it would ever be written. There was always another page someone would add.

\*\*\*

Near St. Augustine

"Hey, Ronnie, I found something."

"What did you find this time little brother? You're always diggin' holes in the sand. What kind of junk are you gonna drag home?

"These. Look. They're pretty. The old box is full of 'em."

"Uh-huh," Donnie said with disgust. "Looks like someone dumped off a box of costume jewelry. Leave it alone."

"It's pirate treasure."

"Naw. That ain't nothin' but junk. Leave it here."

"I'm gonna take a piece and give it to Mom."

Donnie laughed. "Sure. Why not?" he said with sarcasm. "As if Mom doesn't have a dresser full already. She'll make over it real big like she always does when you find something, and then it will disappear among all the rest of the stuff she keeps in the drawers."

"I think it will make her happy."

"Yeah. It can't do any harm. I think it'll make her happy too, little brother. Momma hasn't had too much to be happy about lately."

The End

## WANT TO READ MORE?

*Braddock's Gold Novels – Braddock's Gold, Hunter's Moon, Fool's Wisdom, and Killing Darkness*

*Florida Murder Mystery Novels – Death at Windover, Murder at the Canaveral Diner, and Murder at the Indian River*

*Murder at the Indian River* is the third in the expanding *Florida Murder Mystery Novels*. Each book in the series is written as stand-alone novel. Readers say he keeps getting better. All of Mr. Heavner's seven books can be found on Amazon as ebooks and paperbacks. The first book, *Braddock's Gold*, is also available as an audiobook from Audible at Amazon.

## WANT TO HELP THE AUTHOR?

If you enjoyed the book, would you help get the word out? Please tell others about it. Word-of-mouth advertising is the best marketing tool on this planet.

A good review on Amazon, Goodreads, or elsewhere would help with the author being able to keep writing full time. It doesn't have to be long. Thanks.

## SIGN UP FOR JAY HEAVNER'S NEWSLETTER

With this, Jay will occasionally keep you informed with new books coming out and anything else special. Feel free to email him at jay@jayheavner.com. His website is www.jayheavner.com. He loves reader feedback.

People have asked various questions about my books. While they are all fiction, there are elements of truth to them.

Canaveral Flats does not exist though there is a town with a similar name in the area I indicated. At one time, it did somewhat resemble Canaveral Flats and parts still do. I like to think of it as a cross between Andy Griffith's Mayberry and Al Capp's Dogpatch. You might recognize some of the other places mentioned.

And once, there was a Museum of Sunken Treasure in Cape Canaveral owned by a company that did recover treasure from the 1715 Spanish Treasure Fleet. Like the museum in my book, it was robbed, and the stolen items were never recovered. The Queen's Jewel disappeared when the fleet sank and have never been seen again, but you never know. Someday someone may find them.

If you are interested in knowing more about the 1715 Treasure Fleet, numerous books and articles have been written about it. If you would like to see some of the treasure today, go to Mel Fisher's Treasure Museum in Sebastian, Florida. It's operated by his daughter, Taffi Fisher Abt. It's worth the detour.

Many of the characters in this book are combinations of people I've met and know, but you'll have to figure out which ones, and I'm not telling.

And finding a body in the Indian River is not a rare event. It's a large body of water 156 miles long that popular year round with boaters, fishers, and swimmers, and things do happen.

# BRADDOCK'S GOLD

## by Jay Heavner

## Chapter 1

"Get outta bed, little brother. You told me to get you up when Mom and Dad got up. They're off to work, and you're still sleepin'. Rise and shine, knucklehead."

Robbie heard a groan from under the covers. "Do I have to?"

"You told me to get you up so you could go terrorize those fish in the creek."

"Robbie, I don't feel so good."

"Is it any wonder? I heard you sneakin' around in the kitchen last night. What did you eat?"

"A Twinkie."

"Only a Twinkie?"

"Maybe two."

"What else?"

"A Coke"

"Anything else, Timmy?"

"A candy bar."

"A candy bar."

"But it was a big Baby Ruth."

"It's no wonder you don't feel so good. All that junk food you ate. You're not a billy goat. I hope you learned something from this. The fish are waitin' in fear for your arrival."

"You gonna tell mom, Robbie?"

"No, I think you've been punished enough already. You're not the first kid who did this, little brother. Now, are you gonna get up or not?"

"I'm thinkin' about it."

"Don't think too long, or you'll miss the best fishin' time of the day."

Timmy groaned again as Robbie left his room. If he had known the trouble his discovery would cause, Timmy would have stayed in bed that Friday morn before Memorial Day Weekend in 1995.

The sun rose just past 6:00 a.m. over the small town of Fort Ashby, West Virginia. Tomorrow, crowds of people would leave the big cities of Washington, D.C. and Baltimore, Maryland that were a three-hour drive due east of the little community. They and their families would seek recreation over the long weekend. Some would even find their way to the nearby South Branch of the Potomac and other streams that fed the larger Potomac River as did Patterson Creek.

Little Timmy Miltenberger would be in the third grade when school started in the fall. Today, he planned to fish early that morn, ride his bike up and down the dirt road, and play in the afternoon. His big brother, Robbie aged 16, was supposed to be watching little Timmy.

Mom and Dad would be at their jobs. Timmy had been a shock to his Mom and Dad. It had been eight years since there had been a new child in the home. After five children, the Miltenbergers, good Catholics, thought they had enough, but surprise, surprise! Mary had found herself pregnant with a menopause baby. They loved all their kids, and this one, not planned, would be no different. She and husband Joseph believed all children were gifts from God. They'd laughed how God put them together, yes, Mary and Joseph.

The family joke had been that they'd name their firstborn Jesus. They did in a way, Joshua; the Hebrew-English version of Jesus became the elder's name. Timmy and Robby were the only two still at home, the other siblings grown and off making their own lives. It hadn't been an easy pregnancy for Mary, now an older woman. Tim was born early, a preemie and small, which had led to his nickname, Little Tim, as many people knew him. The doctor said given time, he would catch up, but for now, he was one of the smaller kids in his class of 30.

It was about 7:30 a.m. when he got out of bed. He dressed slowly in his clothes. His tummy still felt funny, but there were fish to be caught. No hand-me-downs for him. The other siblings had those, but he got new, having no one close in age. Into the kitchen he went, got a bowl for corn flakes, poured in some milk, and ate it. He grabbed a banana for a snack, went out the door, and stood on the porch. There, about 40 feet away and down a moderate hill was his delight, Patterson Creek, or just "the crick" as it was known locally. The old house cottage had been there a long time, seen many floods, and had water one foot deep in it back in the 1960s. Then came the great flood of 1985 that one broke all-time records on many streams in the area. Fortunately for the Miltenbergers, back in 1981 their insurance company had required for them to have continued coverage, they must raise their home. The house must be elevated eighteen inches per new government regulations mandated for homes in flood plains. It had been hard times economically for the last few years, and times were still difficult. Mr. Miltenberger contacted several companies for prices. He settled on the contractor that offered to raise the house an additional six inches over the new government requirements for no extra cost, and it was a reasonable price too. Regulations could change again, he said.

This would also move the house to the so-called thousand-year flood level and give more insurance savings. Only once every thousand years was a flood expected at this new level. Joe was glad he did. The flood of 1986 crested a mere two inches below the floor. The pink fiberglass insulation in the floor joists was ruined, but otherwise, the house was unharmed. He replaced it before winter and considered himself lucky compared to what many others in the area suffered, but little Timmy knew none of this. He was born several years afterward, and in his lifetime the creek had behaved itself and remained within its banks, mostly. Last fall when the water had gotten high, the family left for higher ground with relatives, but the stream only threatened, never getting in the house.

He walked over to the shed and opened a wooden box full of decaying leaves, dark soil, and nightcrawlers for fishing. They went in an old can with some of the moist dirt. He stuck the banana in his hip pocket, grabbed his pole, and headed for the creek. It was warm enough for swimming now, but Momma had forbidden it unless someone was there with Timmy, and he listened this time. The stream was a little milky today. His daddy would have said something about it raining upstream, but here, it had been a little dry. He noted some shoe prints in the mud along the creek bank that were quite large. He wondered who had made them this early in the morning.

*Probably that strange old man, Dan Phares, who lived on the neighboring farm.* Timmy was scared of him the first time he'd seen him. His dad had assured him Ole Dan was harmless, though he looked frightening. His dad said Dan had a disability.

Little Tim was not sure what a "disability" was, but he knew he did not want one. Dad also told him he couldn't catch Dan's disability, and that made him feel better. He'd seen Ole Dan walking along the creek several times since then and had spoken to him. Ole Dan seemed a lot smarter than he looked and also a good guy once you got past his weird looks.

Timmy baited his hook with the nightcrawler and threw it in the water. *Good cast.* He liked to go out at night with his flashlight, usually after a rain, and catch the worms. *Find one with the light, walk slowly closer, and grab the part that stuck out of the ground. Don't pull too hard, or you will break it. Hold on, wait for the worm to tire, and then slowly pull it out of the dark soil by the creek.*

By nine, he had a stringer of sunfish, sunnies as he called them, one small bass, and an unknown. Known or not, Momma would fry them up for him. It was time to quit, so he reeled his line in. *Oh great.* He'd snagged something. Old tires, shoes, and assorted trash he'd caught. With a little jerk, the line came free, and he reeled whatever it was through the water. To his surprise, he had a small muddy cloth at the end of his line. *Why, it was a little bag with drawstrings and heavy too.* He emptied the contents in his hand, coins. *One, two, three, a total of 10 quarters. Right size, but the wrong color, yellow. Must be those Indian dollars his first-grade teacher, Mrs. Wilmot, had shown his class.* She had it in her hand in the front of the room, and Timmy sat halfway back, so he didn't get too good a look. One year, she'd passed coins around, and some went missing. She didn't make that mistake again. *Ten coins, ten heavy coins.*

Well, he knew what he would do with one of them tomorrow being Sunday. And another he'd cut up with a hack saw for fishing line sinkers. He could get six or eight pieces from it, and that would be cheaper than buying, and he had this to use already. *Got to clean the fish and then hide my newfound wealth away in his room.* It had been a good day so far for Timmy. He'd wear himself out playing and riding his bike and need a nap later.

"Hey, where you been?" Robbie asked.

"Right here, just got done fishin'," and Timmy held out his catch.

"I thought you're never gonna get out of bed. Looks good. Stay out of trouble." With that, the older brother turned and went back into the house.

*Yup, looks like it's gonna be a good summer though nothin' excitin' ever happens 'round here.*

Jay Heavner

www.ingramcontent.com/pod-product-compliance
Lightning Source LLC
Chambersburg PA
CBHW020633250626
47154CB00008B/2659